MW01043385

FUN WITH RAINBOWS

GARETH OWENS

IMMERSION PRESS

SUSSEX, ENGLAND, UK

Published in Great Britain by Immersion Press, 2010

ISBN 978-0-9563924-0-4

Stories copyright © Gareth Owens, 2010

For my Dad
David Caradoc Owens
1936 – 2008

Acknowledgements

"Across the Sea of No Return" first published in *Mallorn*, the Journal of the Tolkien Society, Spring 2008

"Ignorantia Juris" first published in *Nature*, 17th July 2008

"A New Note for Nate" first published in *Nature*, 30th August 2007

"Frog in a Bucket" first published in *Nature Physics,* October 2007

"Liquid Skin" first published in *The West Pier Gazette and Other Stories* from Three Legged Fox Books, UK, 2007

"It's a Temple" first published in *Ruins: Terra* from Hadley Rille Books, 2007

"Tick Tock Curley Wurley" First published in *Nature*, 7th September 2006

All other stories published here for the first time.

Contents

FORWARD
by Henry Gee

It was a decade ago, now, that *Nature*, the international weekly journal of science, decided to start a new venture. To celebrate the upcoming millennium (it was 1999 - do at least *try* to keep up, at the back) we thought we'd publish, in a small way, what some people call 'Science Fiction'. Ignoring those wags (mostly scientists whose papers we'd rejected) who said that 'Everything *Nature* publishes is science fiction', we went ahead, with a new, original story from Arthur C. Clarke, which appeared in our 130th anniversary issue, 4 November, 1999.

As the editor of *Nature*'s SF output, I soon learned that SF to many scientists is as the air we breathe - and that a great deal of talent lurks out there, untapped. Whereas once *Nature*'s SF stories were on a commission-only basis, I decided to open the doors to all comers. The floodgates opened.

Since then I've published stories about lesbian robots from a senior citizen in Alaska; the colonization of Mars from an academic virologist in Singapore; and colourful dialogue from a teenage girl in Omaha, Nebraska. *Nature* has always taken mentoring seriously in science, but it works, too, for fiction - for although many of *Nature*'s SF authors are established names in the field, many more have just begun their voyages into writing - and, for some, *Nature* represents their first ever SF sale. What keeps me going as an editor is the thought that, one day, an author will step up to accept a Hugo or a Nebula and say something like 'if it weren't for that nice man at *Nature* who bought my first story ...'

Gareth Caradoc Owens, to give him his full appellation, palaeolinguist, wizard and writer of rare facility, was one of those authors who came out of nowhere. As you'll see from this collection, he is a scribe of some versatility, and I'm privileged to have been able to have published five of his stories, all of which appear in this collection - four for *Nature* (and its sister publication, *Nature Physics*, which ran SF under my watch for a couple of years) - and one, a fantasy, for *Mallorn*, the Journal of the Tolkien Society, which I also edit. And so, without further ado...

Dr Henry Gee, Senior Editor, *Nature*
Cromer, Norfolk, July 2009

A NEW NOTE FOR NAT

Nat used to be in a band. Until yesterday that was. That's him, sat in the armchair, the unhappy looking one talking to Midge. And there's Duffy and Slingshot. And that's me in the other corner.

You can't always see me on the screen, Tim was holding the camera. I'm only the agent, and it was the band we wanted to catch that day. This was a promo, backstage thing they wanted to put on the website. You know the type of clip, "Get interactive with the guys".

This was taken about three years ago, back in the day when Invisible Ear was the biggest band on three continents. You must have been living under a rock to have missed them, even if you couldn't actually hear anything they did. They were on the crest of a wave, first of a new breed, pioneers on the new frontier, and I can honestly say that I've never heard a single note that they've ever played. Not that I'm that bothered, they have made me a very happy man over the last few years. M. Osborne agent to the stars, known to one and all as Mozzy. I have bands queuing up for me now, and I owe it all to Nat and the gang.

However, there would have been no Invisible Ear at all, no career for Nat, or for me, if it hadn't been for an irritated shopkeeper.

The problem this guy had was he wanted to discourage the gangs of youngsters from hanging around outside his shop without putting off his paying customers. His solution was to put a buzzing box by the door that made an irritating high-pitched sound that only the youngsters could hear. 'Dults lose their hearing from the top down, so the older customers could come in and spend money without any problem, but anyone under the age of about eighteen would have this constant buzz, like toothache. Really put them off.

Well, kids ain't stupid. They took to this idea that there's stuff they can hear that the 'dults can't and made it their own. Suddenly there were ring-tones for cell phones just for them, and that was when Nat and Slingshot had the idea to get together and begin Invisible Ear. They started writing tunes in this register. A music that was theirs and theirs alone, no grown-ups allowed, 'dults keep-out.

I was an agent, always on the lookout for the next big thing, and I saw Invisible Ear play at a school hall. I wasn't expecting much. School bands are usually awful, shouting boys doing covers of angry music, but this was something else. Nat raised his hands in the air, counted the band in with a "one two three", and they started to play. The audience went wild. I could see heads bobbing up and down, and they danced around to this invisible beat, and yet I could hear nothing, nada, zip and zilch.

I stood amazed and puzzled, for the next three minutes the band played, and Nat sang (he recorded vocals prior, pitch shifted them up and then mimed so it looked like he was singing). Then they stopped. The hall, which had been silent while the band played, erupted into wild shouts of unrestrained enthusiasm.

I signed them like a shot. For the first time, there was a band I could represent, that I didn't actually have to listen to.

But the real fun was taking the demo around to record companies, playing these ultrasonic songs to the guys in suits, and then telling them that only cool people could hear the music. Hans Christian Anderson would have loved it.

Screwing their faces up with concentration they'd lean forward and then they would nod, and look like they were getting into it, and about half the time Nat hadn't switched the player on.

Invisible Ear took the world by storm. Not only music but vids, games and online worlds; Japanese children would queue for hours just to get the latest Ear game to play at home. They became a worldwide cultural phenomenon.

Then yesterday, at the height of the band's fame and popularity, they sacked Nat. He's too old you see. He sat in that chair there and the poor kid was almost in tears; he's been wearing hearing aids for the last six months. He was totally distraught, been tryin' to hold off the inevitable, but what can you do? He's over the hill four months before his eighteenth birthday. I told him, "Nobody can keep time at bay, not even you Nat. You founded a club meant to keep grown-ups out, and then you grew up, sorry."

I let him wallow for a while, but to be honest what kind of agent would I be if I hadn't seen this coming?

"Look, Nat. Take those silly things off your ears, you are not going deaf." I didn't give him the choice. I walked over to where he sat and pulled the hearing aids off his ears. He yelped a bit. "Like I said, you founded a club for the youth market, but you're not the only one getting older. The record company is beginning to get complaints that the recordings they made of Invisible Ear's songs have faded. Your fans are putting on your music, and they can't hear it any more. It's not the songs that are fading, but your first lot of fans are about the same age as you, so they can press the play button as much as they like but nothing's gonna come out, at least not for them any more."

"So?" he said.

"It's time for Nat to grow up and go solo," I said grinning. "To transpose all your songs into an audible register, re-record them as a series of duets with the hottest stars, and get your fans to buy them all over again. Welcome to the 'dults Nat, I think you'll find it much more fun than you were expecting."

ONE MAN WENT TO MOW

Growing up, Kilburn's father had often taken him and his brother out to the wild forest. All that the two boys wanted to do was run and play and fight. In those far off days Kilburn remembered his father would occasionally stop them with a raised finger to say, "Shhh... Listen. What do you hear?" The boys would stand still, briefly, irritated at the intrusion into their self-contained, adult free zone. They would listen intently, but all they could ever hear was the sound of the freezing wind and their own thumping pulse, loud in their ears.

"I can't hear anything," Kilburn would say.

"Yes you can. You can hear the silence." The young Kilburn would then look up at his father with one of those "don't be stupid dad" faces, and go back to screaming like a racing engine, driving back into the kingdom of imagination.

That childhood was long ago, in a different quieter century, and now Kilburn the grown man understood what his father had meant.

He lived in a Kentish dormitory village, commuting each day to where he worked in London. The background grumble of traffic was his constant metronome, marking the daily stresses and the life stealing worries of his existence. The sound from the motorway, five miles to the north, never subsided. Even at three in the morning there was always the far off rumble of the forever lorries, and above the perpetual earthquake of the road, the intermittent sky filling roar of distant jets going to full flaps.

However, on one day of the year, Kilburn had discovered that if he stood at the end of his drive he could experience silence; sometimes for as long as two minutes at a time.

On Christmas Day, he would take the hand of his own son and lead him outside. They would sit on the bonnet of his car and look at the bare branches of the ash trees silhouetted against the white skies of mid-winter.

Every few minutes a car would go past, and they would listen to the sound of the tyres fading into the distance. They could follow these individual cars as they drove, plotting their path through the centre of the village as accurately as any sonar. Gradually the noise would fade towards inaudibility and they would get a tantalising promise of silence. They could hear that the motorway was dead, there were no aircraft above them, and sometimes there would be the sound of a world without vehicles.

It was in these silences that Kilburn realised that the world used to be still. For billions of years the only sounds were those that the Earth made when she was singing to herself; the breeze through the branches, and the surf smashing the mountains into sandy submission.

That precious period of Christmas Day silence had dwindled; until three or four years ago there was always an overlap between the fading car and the next one coming along. Kilburn felt bereft. It was as if those one or two minutes of silence charged up his batteries for the entire year, and without them he was unable to shift the knot of tension that made his neck crack and crick whenever he moved suddenly.

However, today was different. The June sun was cool and weak in the early morning, as if it was saving itself for its midday passion. Kilburn had taken the day off. He made breakfast and stumbled around the kitchen as he assembled his awareness. This was the first day of the new silence. This was the first day that it was actually illegal to use a hydrocarbon powered vehicle on the road.

He listened to the Today programme with a glass of too sharp orange juice in his hand, trying to exercise self control like a child trying not to unwrap a present, but he was unequal to the struggle.

He took his glass and wandered barefoot out through his front door, down the path and leaned over the five-bar gate that formed the border of his world.

The swaddling of sound that enveloped him was onion-skinned in depth and complexity. As he stood he was able to peel back each layer and find fainter sounds underneath as he headed into the heart of the soundscape. The main theme was the dying rumble of a 747 heading out across the Atlantic. Quiet and distant, but its vast howl lay behind everything. Kilburn patient, waited for the airliner to stamp it carbon footprint on someone else's face, and eventually the rumble fell below the audible horizon.

And there it was, just briefly, the sound of a world gone quiet. Birdsong, individual and different: a nightingale singing during the day; wood-pigeon, the drum-and-bass of avian music; below that Kilburn became aware of the twitter of the always angry sparrows, and below that the perma-buzz of the insect world, and then…

Brrr….brrrr….Brrrr. Down the road a ways the sound of one of his neighbours trying to start a chainsaw. Brrrr…brrrr..Ong-ong-ongongong…Aaaaaaaaaaaaaaaaaaaw… ongongong…Aaaaaaaaaw..aaaw…ong-ong-ong- onk-pfrr. Kilburn sighed. Slumped, he turned and went back into the house. He would try again in an hour or so, when the ear-ringing branch lopper had got fed up.

He perfumed the house with the aroma of good coffee and his wife returned from the school run like a spirit summoned by incense. They kissed good-naturedly and split a copy of the Telegraph between them. Kilburn sat for a few minutes but was unable to concentrate on the problems of the world.

With a flouncy and satisfyingly noisy crinkle of newsprint he threw the paper down on the Davenport and stood to look out of the French-windows. He could still faintly hear the chainsaw through the glass. He sighed, and wandered listlessly out into the hall.

There was no thought in his actions, the mixture of anticipation and disappointment mingled like explosive chemicals in his brain. He stood by the front door looking out through the porthole. Without being aware that he was doing so, he had balled his fist and was gently rapping the wall beside him. The rhythm was insistent and at just the correct frequency to trip his wife's "For God's Sake" threshold.

"For God's sake Kilburn, just go outside will you? You're cluttering up the place."

"Hmmm," he replied, not really paying any attention, but her words were enough for him to open the door and drift outside again.

He mooched down to the gate and took his accustomed position of thought, elbows on the crosspiece, chin on his palms. The chainsaw still snarled out its hatred of trees, and as Kilburn watched the road, he became aware of the eerie stream of traffic. The electric cars made no noise other than the sound of their tyres on the road and a high pitched whine that was above the ability of his middle-aged ears to pick up. So as the cars, familiar in shape, trundled by, they seemed to Kilburn almost like automotive ghosts. A wild hunt made from the spirits of the dead V8s.

Suddenly with a final cat-with-a-fur-ball spit, the chainsaw choked into silence. There was a bit of a rumble of road noise, but that died as soon as the car was out of sight.

And there it was again. The trees shivered in the breeze, but it was a local, natural, noise. There was a deep stillness beyond. Kilburn suddenly realised that the ever present rumble of London was gone. He had lived with the noise of the great city all his life, never even noticing it until the day it died.

The silence squeezed his belly. It felt like fingers around his bowels.

Brrr…Brrr…bub…bub..bub.bubbububububububub…raaaaaaaaaaaaaa…… A chainsaw had obviously proved not noisy enough for his neighbour. The lawn mower rattled into eccentric life. But Kilburn was patient; how long could it take to mow a lawn?

Twenty minutes later he was still frozen to the spot. It had become a contest of wills. However, in some freak aberration of health and safety, mower man had apparently got a machine that would allow him to keep the engine running at full throttle even while he left it to empty the grass-box.

The noxious fume spouting, petrol-guzzling, Gaia killing automechanical monsters of the twentieth century had finally been slain by the cold economic blade of the twenty-first. The roads belonged to the electrics and the price of aviation fuel had pushed flying back into the realms of the clouds for most people. Vast sailing vessels once more claimed the seas, but as he stood listening for a silence that lay just beyond the veil of two-stroke, Kilburn realised that the man next door could run that lawnmower all day. It never occurred to Kilburn that his neighbour might be scared of the vast silence that loomed, holding it at bay like a frightened caveman keeping back the darkness with a flaming torch.

Forty-five minutes Kilburn stood there as if queuing, patient, waiting for the man with the mower to finish, but there was a growing warmth in his face. Every two minutes or so he would look down at his watch and his nostrils would flare a little and he would huff. This was beginning to feel like a very personal attack. After all, he had taken the day off. This was his special treat. All he wanted was to stand and enjoy the first properly silent day since the invention of the internal combustion engine.

How could that be too much to ask? Every day he had submerged himself in the human roar of the city, and had through years of diesel-belching clattering buses, clogged roads and pneumatic drills, managed to claw himself a little space in the countryside. And now, when it was time to enjoy that hard fought for silence, mower man was stealing it from him.

Kilburn stood rigid. His arms were now held stiffly at his sides, the hands clenched into white-knuckled fists. One hour and fifteen minutes he stood like that. There had been a brief respite at fifty-seven minutes, but it just turned out to be a forty-five second break for refuelling.

Suddenly everything in Kilburn relaxed. He realised that he was grinning. He turned and walked into the house, his fingers did not even fumble with the keys on the cabinet as he got the Purdey. It was a beautiful over and under 12-bore with thirty-inch barrels and a Turkish Walnut stock.

With the gun broken over his right forearm, he strolled down the lane, following the sound of his prey. He walked up the drive of a white painted bungalow that he had never previously noticed, past the greenhouse, and out onto the back lawn. The man with the mower was fat, balding, in his early sixties and wearing a pair of shorts and a vest. He looked up as Kilburn approached, and as soon as they made eye contact Kilburn brought the gun up and cocked it without even breaking stride.

Kilburn thought that he moved quite quickly for someone of his age. The man in the vest turned and ran straight towards the back door of his house.

Kilburn ignored him. He walked up to the mower and levelled the gun at the middle of its engine. He gently squeezed the trigger, there was a single loud report, and the top of the mower disintegrated in an oily black explosion. Finally there was an ear ringing silence. The tinnitus caused by the shot wore off as Kilburn sauntered slowly back towards his gate. He savoured every second of that vast, delicious silence in the fifteen minutes before the sirens started.

ACROSS THE SEA OF NO RETURN

The dream was the same every night, settling on his shoulders heavy as the northern snows. They had come to him in the winter, these silent ravens of his nightly vision. They stood guard over his sleep, their vigil unbroken, unexplained and unwelcome.

Lludan had travelled far since leaving the great cities of his homeland. The last year that he could remember the name for was "Year of the Golden Throne". He only knew that because it was the name of the festival during which he had left Karduniash to go wandering.

Ten times since then the sun had passed through the Bull of Heaven, the sign of his birth, and he had travelled further from "The Gods' Gateway" than any civilised man had ever been.

He had learned the ways of the sword from the Ashuriyya, he had learned the ways of the horse in Washukani, he had learned the ways of the sea from the Kaltiyya, and always he was drawn to the west.

Travelling from the shores of the Lower Sea, he had sailed beyond the Upper Sea, journeying into the Third Sea - the Sea of no Return.

Lludan is what his rescuers named him, unable as they were to pronounce his given name. A joke in the local tongue about his size, he bore it with good grace for in the speech of the old ones it meant 'Mighty Man'. He stood a full head above everyone that he had met on the Isle of Tin.

Strangers were not always welcome amongst the inhabitants of the Isle, who were known as the tribes of the Daen. After the angry seas had thrown Lludan against the razor sharp black rocks of the Isle, he had escaped the waves only to nearly die of the cold as he clung to life against the fury of the storm. The sons of the Daen had found him and he did not resist as they took his sword from where he had fastened it over his shoulder. Then they led this shaggy giant at spear-point before the head of the clan of Mael.

Lludan, shivering with the cold, knew that without the local tongue he needed to find a way to show his worth. In the longhouse of the village, one of the small war ponies stood placidly by the seat of judgement.

Lludan slipped his bonds, and with a move as lithe as the salmon leap he crossed the floor to the pony. His guards raised their spears ready to bring him down but the headman waved the warriors back.

Lludan looked around and, on seeing that he was being given room to perform, bent down low and placed his neck and shoulders under the belly of the pony. With a great scream he lifted the surprised little horse until he, Lludan, stood with his back straight as an Ashuriyyan arrow and a ferocious look in his eyes. In his weakened state the effort nearly killed him. He could feel muscles in his back being pulled and ripped. The pain was as massive as the weight of the pony but his agony merely added to the ferocity of his expression.

The old grey-bearded headman smiled and laughed. The potential of such a mighty ally was not lost on him, or the rest of the clan. As this giant of a man stood silhouetted against the flames of the fire in the long house, the chief nodded to himself.

*

The clan of Mael accepted Lludan, and without their kindness he would not have survived his first winter in the ice. He took up the local custom of dressing in garments of fur and the closely woven cloth of the Bolgea. They even made a round house for him within the village wall, and that had been when the dream started.

He would wake, eyes wide and panting, to find two large birds, one on each shoulder. He had seen nothing like them before he had arrived on the isle but here they were common, large, black, and as shiny as the shell of a beetle. Their loud colonies were like towns in the trees. They called the darkness down at the end of the day and their raucous voices carried on the still and chill air. Yet the two that woke him every night, made no noise. He lay on his back, and they hovered with their great sharp beaks one over each of his eyes.

They said nothing, they made no sound. They merely looked into his soul. Then he would wake a second time, realising that the birds were the spirits of dream. Unlike in normal dreams the birds stayed with him for the whole of the waking day. He could feel their presence with him wherever he walked.

The winter passed and the thin sunlight of the northern spring began to warm the lands. Icy melt waters ran swiftly off the mountains, swelling streams into furious cataracts. The new year was come, winter was dead and the cycle of rituals was set to begin anew. Over the dark months Lludan had listened to the tongue of the sons of Mael, learning to talk a few words as a child does.

The headman of the village had earned the battle name Straight Spear. His hair was long and still mostly black. He wore it unbound as was the tradition amongst the people of the isle. His beard was grey and a jagged and dark scar ran up one cheek, stopping before the miraculously uninjured eye, and then continuing through his brow.

Straight Spear came to Lludan one morning and informed him that they were to travel with the livestock of the clan to the village of Cadri'ell. The spell weavers there would make the fires of spring and the annual marriages would be blessed or abandoned.

Lludan welcomed the trip. He felt that perhaps he would be able to lose the two black spirits of his dream. They gathered supplies for the journey, which would take two days of easy travelling. Easy travelling, that was, for everyone else in the party, but not for Lludan.

A giant of a man was not made for travel on the back of the ponies of the Isle of Tin; therefore he walked.

"Tell me of the fires of spring," he called to Straight Spear on the morning of the second day. They meandered slowly, following their animals through the well-trodden pathways of the deep forest path that led to Cadri'ell.

Straight Spear Smirked, and made a sound like an owl.

"Hooo," he said, "this place is the home of the green, and when the winter dies, the green comes again in the spring. The lamb and the goat, the cow and the maiden, are linked with the fertility of these lands. This is the celebration of the rebirth of the world. The livestock is driven between the fires, and the contracts of marriage are made solemn, and more to the point there is much drinking."

"Much drinking?" asked Lludan hopefully.

"*Much* drinking!" came the emphatic reply.

"Straight Spear!" A shout went up from the front of the herd. The old chief looked up and saw that the group had come to a halt. In the path stood a single figure, confident and leaning on the stout handle of a long axe. Its small blade told Lludan that it was better at going through heads than trees. Straight Spear rode casually and unhurriedly to speak to the figure.

"How many cows you takin'?" asked the bandit.

"Thirty-five," said Straight Spear.

"We'll take fifteen," said the bandit.

"I'll suggest a wager," said Straight Spear. He was relaxed and exuded confidence. "My champion against yours, winner takes all, our cattle against your weapons. What d'you say?"

The bandit looked off into the woods and called out.

"What say you Brays, a battle of champions?"

A great shout came as answer.

"Hah! Farmers all, nary a warrior amongst the lot of them." A barrel-chested fig-ure emerged from the bracken. His limbs were stout as any carthorse and the muscles that wound around his forearms resembled a sinuous snake writhing beneath the skin. This was not mere strength for show. He walked confidently down to join his lieutenant.

"Send your best out, old man," he said, "and I'll personally teach you the difference between a warrior and a cow worrier." Brays flung his cloak aside and snatched the axe from the grasp of the first bandit.

"Lludan, it's time to earn your keep," Straight Spear called out, although his gaze never broke from that of the bandit chief.

Lludan walked slowly up the line of cattle, until he stood before Brays. With one hand he slipped the knot of his cloak and threw it to Straight Spear for safekeeping. The gilded pommel of his long sword Sikatsayli, a final gift from Pool priest of SharAn, rose above his shoulder.

In a single liquid move Lludan reached up and grasped the sword, bringing it forward, liberating it from its carrying rings and aligning the point so that the entire length of the blade was now directed at the eyes of the bandit.

Brays looked up, and his face registered exactly how far up he was having to look.

"Bound by honour now you are," reminded Straight Spear, his voice filled with gentle humour.

Lludan looked at the axe. He had learned to treat axes with a great deal of respect. The shortest fight he had ever seen had been between an Aki'iyya swordsman and his friend, Tarhunda the Luwian, at the battle of 'iluseh.

The two warriors had stood assessing each other. Tarhunda had brought down the end of the axe handle on the unprotected toes of his opponent, and as the swordsman hopped about comically on one foot, Tarhunda, with a single swipe of his bearded axe, hooked the remaining supporting ankle, pulling it out from under the Aki'iyya so that the unfortunate soldier was sent to the ground on his back, from which he did not get up again.

Ludan looked at Brays, judging the grip with which he held the haft. His right hand was slightly too close to the head, and his grip was slightly too spread out; also Lludan noticed that Brays had all his weight on the back foot, and that his legs were too straight. This was an opponent that had never been taught how to fight, everything he had learned came from experience, and judging by the web of scarring that covered every visible patch of skin he was a slow learner.

The two men stood looking into each other's eyes, weighing up their adversary. Suddenly Lludan saw the moment that he had been waiting for. The bandit Brays blinked, and as he opened his eyes again the focus of his gaze had slightly changed. Lludan lifted one of his feet and planted a great kick into the chest of the surprised bandit chief, sending him spinning backwards.

The kick had the desired effect and when Brays turned back to face Lludan the rage burned in his eyes. He rushed the much larger man and, once within reach, he took a brutal overhead swing with his axe.

The attack was inexpert and easily sidestepped. Brays flew passed and Lludan deftly reached out to grasp the handle of the axe. In the same motion, with an extended ankle he tripped Brays so that the bandit came crashing to the ground, deprived of both weapon and dignity.

Stunned, the bandit took a second to realise that he was lying on the floor, and that was all the time that Lludan needed. Placing one foot in the middle of the bandit's back, he raised Sikatsayli's deadly curved blade over Brays' head.

"No! Lludan!" shouted Straight Spear, staying the swing. "They did not attack us, they did not demand the whole herd, and they accepted the terms of an honourable wager. If you take this man's life, you will dishonour the clan of Mael. Now Brays, order your men to bring down their weapons."

Brays, pinned into the mud, began to laugh.

"Men?" he said. "Men! It's just me and my brother. There are no men, and you already have our axe." Lludan was not yet that fluent with the tongue and Brays had an accent that made the words difficult for him to understand, but eventually he realised what the bandit was saying. He had made a fool of him, made him fight when there was no need of it. He felt the rage rising in him in a way that he had not during the mêlée.

The muscles in his arm tensed, the great sword was once more about to begin its downward sweep, when Lludan became aware of a noise. It was the sound of laughter. Straight Spear was laughing, a great warm and deep laugh that came from the heart; it was the same laugh that had saved his own life a few short months before.

"Fearless beggars! Ride with us, and share a meal. Your blood shall not stain our hands today. Lludan put up your weapon." Lludan, confused, did as he was bid. Reluctantly he moved aside and let Brays up.

After that the remainder of the journey through the close-packed forest passed smoothly, if rather grumpily on Lludan's part.

By nightfall they came to the place where forest met plains. The sound of wild music could be heard coming from a large settlement nearby. Behind the great wooden palisade of Cadri'ell, the flickering of many campfires showed, orange and smoky, making the shadows of dancers rise into the evening, spiralling up as though to dance among the stars.

The travellers from Maelgoyd were welcomed as long lost brothers. The tall warhorns were sounded in greeting from the gates and the herd was taken off to pasture. Brays the bandit and his brother Maiv were handed drinking cups full of the dark, sweet mead so beloved of the peoples of the Isle. The feast was in full swing with musicians filling the air with melodies that were as gentle as the breeze and as wild as the passion that grips the lover.

Lludan tapped Straight Spear on the shoulder, none too gently, for he was still upset over Brays.

"Much drinking?" he said.

"Aye, little Llu, much drinking, and some good eating too." The answer was not what Lludan had been after.

"Much drinking… Now." Straight Spear got the point. A place was made for them at the feast and Lludan received a brimming cup of mead from the great cauldron. A shiny and sticky hunk of meat was placed in his hands and for the first time in months Lludan was happy. A haunch of venison, a cup of mead, only one more thing was needed to make this moment perfect for him. Grinning happily, he looked around.

Suddenly the music stopped, the sounds of the celebration ceased, the dancers all froze in their places. Beyond the timid sputtering of the cooking fire, she stood, beautiful and proud. Her hair seemed to be flame itself, her eyes green flashing emeralds that possessed life beyond that imparted to them by the fire. Her skin was as pale as the fresh snow that blanketed the distant mountain tops, and her gaze went through Lludan as if he had been harpooned. The moment stretched, and for all that she was proud Lludan felt in her a vulnerability. She needed him.

He blinked and she was gone. The revels around him were pallid now compared to a few moments before, mere passionless shadows compared to the reality of the full-bloodied beauty that had just appeared to him. He sat for a moment, shocked. He had seen many things in his wanderings, he had been with many people but never had a woman so shaken him to the core. He had to find her. He stood and walked to the place where she had pierced him deeper than any sword. He looked around for some sign of her but she had disappeared.

He returned to where Straight Spear sat and in halting words he asked about the woman. The headman of the clan of Mael shrugged.

"There are many pretty girls here, from all the clans. Look around, you'll find her." Lludan stood, his cup forgotten. The only thought in him now was to find the mysterious beauty that had put a glamour on him.

He wandered away from the firelight, away from the feast and the music into the darkened part of the village. Everyone was at the celebration and as he walked deeper into the darkness the shouts and laughter dwindled behind him, and he could feel the cool air of the night sky and the damp rich grass beneath his feet. The roundhouses of Cadri'ell smelled of the peat of the fires.

Lludan felt a hollowness inside him, the same feeling that he would get before a battle. He reached up and touched the pommel of Sikatsayli for reassurance. He was now crouched over almost double. Unconsciously he had begun to behave as if in an enemy's camp. He stretched his head around the wall of one of the round houses and heard the gentle low murmuring of a whispered conversation between two men.

A small fire before them, the two warriors stood in easy conversation. Yet Lludan was able to see from their posture that both were alert and ready to fight. Her eyes burning emeralds, her skin pale as the snow. She was inside and not an army of all the great empires would keep Lludan from her side. He had to find her.

Silent as his years of experience had taught him to be, he worked his way through the unattended buildings until he came to the back of the guarded house. Quietly as he could he pulled Sikatsayli clear of her rings, and with his ears straining to catch the murmuring of the guards he began to cut through the thatch of the building.

The rhythm of the conversation did not waver and Lludan worked his way through the grass and the reed hurdles of the wall. He cut with the point of his sword until he had made a hole big enough to peer through. The scene inside the round house showed him what he already knew. She was there, this vision of all things feminine. He managed to get an arm through the hole, and then a shoulder, until he tumbled through onto the straw of a bed that was made next to the wall.

The gloom of the space was emphasised by two torches that hung from the upright beams that supported the domed roof. The floor was bare, just made from the hard packed black soil. Between the beams, she stood, and where everything else in the world was dark and drained, she radiated colour as if she was the only thing real.

Her clothes were as red as fresh blood, and her feet were bare.

"You came," she said.

"When you call I will always come," said Lludan in his own tongue.

"I know," she replied.

Lludan looked down and noticed two prostrate bodies curled like puppies on a rug.

"My magic may not kill," she said gently as she saw him notice her guards. "They sleep for now."

"Come, we must leave," said Lludan, indicating the hole he had made in the wall. He turned back, expecting her to follow him, but she stood still. Instead she pointed at the ground.

Lludan noticed for the first time a thin ring that encircled her. On the floor around her, in a perfect circle, was placed a ring of feathers from the hooded crow, and both inside and outside of the ring was another unbroken circle of salt.

"They hold me captive, and they force me to do their bidding," she said. "The villagers of Cadri'ell have taken their wealth from gifts that have been stolen, and power that has been taken against my will." She looked into his eyes and Lludan felt as if a torrent of flame flowed into him. She was beyond all mortal desire, his passion for her burned inside; not like the poets' fire, imagined and weak, but like the blade pulled from the forge and pressed against the skin.

"Break the circle Lu Gal, Gnir Nita Kalamgha." She spoke the tongue of the old ones. Lludan knelt down before her, and with his hands he scrabbled at the earth, pushing the feathers aside, and breaking the circles of salt.

Suddenly he felt a gentle hand on his shoulder, and he stood to find that she was already behind him.

"Leave the way you came, and make straight for the forest, I will meet you there." Lludan was entirely in the thrall of this creature, and although the idea of parting, even for a moment, was more painful than any wound he had ever endured, he made no word of complaint.

He slipped out through the hole in the wall and made for the palisade. Everyone was still at the feast, and only a few warriors patrolled the platform behind the village walls. It was no effort for Lludan to swarm up one of the pilings, and leap over the wall and disappear into the darkness of the forest.

He wandered aimlessly for a measureless time, his thoughts chaotic and confused. Turning his back on Cadri'ell, he stumbled into the darkness. He breasted the rise of a small hill and in a hollow on the other side, out of sight of the village, he found her. She sat bright as the fire she had already made in the bracken lined hollow.

In trance Lludan came to her. She held out her hand to him, and he took it. Wordlessly they came together, and for the first time in his life Lludan understood how incomplete a man is.

The fire died and Lludan slept with her wrapped in his arms. In his slumber he felt her stir, and he awoke with his eyes wide. Before him were the two ravens of his dream, between them the woman that had taken his soul and heart. He could not move. She walked towards him, and where he lay powerless on the ground, she kissed him. She kissed him above his heart, she kissed each of his hands, she kissed him on his throat, she kissed his mouth, and she kissed his forehead. Slowly, her gaze locked with his. She stepped backwards, until she once more stood between the silent birds.

For a second Lludan was able to see them as they really were: an old woman with a spindle stood on the left, and on the right a fearsome warrior woman armed as for battle. Then like drifting smoke, there were three of the birds. They turned and flew into the stars of the night sky, cawing as they went.

Lludan woke a second time. She was gone. He stood and faced the dawn alone. Turning his back to the rising sun he began to walk back to Cadri'ell.

There was still something of the dream within him. She had left something of her spirit inside him, and he knew that he would never be entirely alone again. Her last gift to him had been to bestow upon him a new name. He was now the one called Gwion. He had been reborn in the rising sun and his path wound ever to the west. He knew that he would not tarry on the Isle of Tin for much longer, and that somewhere across the Sea of No Return his destiny awaited him.

The breeze caressing his face, as if from a raven's wing, Gwion set his path towards the west and to the future.

INNOCENT PROMETHEUS

There is no such thing as "tactical" genetic warfare.
Gen. Su Zi Yip Chief of Staff, New American Federation b2123 - d2165

Kow's breasts were full of eyes. They formed deep in her mammary tissue, like cysts. As they grew bigger they filled with fluid, and once completely formed they migrated out to where they split her skin and peered sightlessly at the world.

Monitor Alice Dare looked at the pathetic creature before her. Something that had once been human, now twisted into the new flesh. She hefted the weight of the control box in her hands. All over the mutie's body eyes had erupted through the skin - her shoulders and arms, her hands, even the ends of her fingers. The skin split away like peeling sunburn and something looked through from inside, and not all of those eyes were human. Alice knew that there were no nerves behind them, but somehow they tracked her as she moved about, making her preparations.

The New American Consortium, in the person of Monitor Alice Dare, kept Kow naked. Clothing, she reasoned, could injure the delicate tissues that were to be harvested from this hapless victim of the first G-War. She had also been restrained since Alice had noticed the ring of scar tissue around Kow's wrist. This had been where the desperate mutie had taken the point of a carelessly mislaid screwdriver and tried to rub out the bracelet of shiny black rodent eyes and their accompanying clusters of twisted rat's teeth that had burst through her skin.

Alice pressed a stud on the heavy control box and a microphone extended on a boom from the ceiling.

"Monitor Alice Dare, resumption of routine organ retrieval from the mutie known as Kow. Status update: the fears concerning mutation stability and transgenic cross contamination in organ recipients have been adjudged to be baseless, however as a precaution only the crystal lens will be used from each eye retrieved from Kow. This is until the definitive base sequence of the viral carrier and the modified PAX6 weapon can be established."

Kow was hunkered down in the corner, squatting like a fearful foetus, her arms raised as if against the light. It had been just over three years since she had wandered into Consortium territory looking for help, and they looked after her bodily needs and her health as much as they needed to. Her blonde hair was kept clean and shoulder length, not because the Consortium was showing any pity, but because the order to have her head shaved went missing somewhere along the chain of command.

Alice had inherited Kow eighteen months before, when her previous keeper walked out into the Radlands and never came back, and this harvesting had become a daily ritual.

The yellow box of the control pad was attached to the ceiling by a heavy duty power tether. Alice became aware of what she was going to do next, and a flush of excitement blushed trembling warm in her belly. Deliberately she held down the big green button, and a large electrical whining, winding noise began in the floor above. The chain around Kow's neck began to be reeled in upwards and those at her ankles disappeared like fleeing snakes into the holes in the concrete floor. The wrists of the mutie were stretched out sideways until Kow was held in an erect star, completely unable to move.

Alice became aware of whimpering.

"Be quiet. Or it's the mirror," she hissed. The sound ceased, with deliberately pursed lips, although tears now streamed from the perfect blue eyes of her face - the only functioning eyes on her. Alice had often thought of harvesting those but discovered that the threat of her own reflection was the greatest punishment that she could offer this genetic casualty. It had become something of a game for Alice, and now the idea of depriving Kow of her sight never crossed the Monitor's mind.

"Visual surveillance of extremities," Alice spoke into the microphone.

With a dispassionate gaze she tracked over the pale skin of the young mutie, and where her eyes travelled her fingers followed. Down the inside of Kow's right thigh she found what she was looking for, a new vine of eyes had broken the surface of the skin, erupting like galls. They were in a lattice formation, each human eye nested between two sets of rodent eyes arranged in a double row. These were good ones, Alice noted. They had formed lids and tear ducts.

Alice stroked them, running her hand up the line of them. It was an odd sensation. Simultaneously feeling the smooth flesh of Kow's thigh but as her fingers reached each eye they closed under her touch, the perfectly formed lashes an answering caress. The whole time she was doing this she fixed her gaze on the terrified face of Kow.

There was a physical symmetry between the two women, both were blonde with fair skin and blue eyes, but within their faces two very different spirits peered out from behind the doors of the soul.

Careless now of the invasive nature of her touch, Alice circled the topmost eye on Kow's thigh with the tip of her middle finger. She moved so close to her completely restrained victim that she could feel the warmth of her skin through the thin material of her shirt. There was a hushed moment where both women waited, each knowing what would happen next, one holding her breath in dread, one in excitement.

"I'll take those," hissed Alice, and her fingers, so gentle a second before, plunged into the flesh of the helpless woman. These eyes had no protective socket of bone to keep them safe. Alice pinched the orb between her thumb and forefinger, feeling it like a marble in the flesh. She pushed hard until it popped, wet and bloody into her palm. Kow gasped and muttered the one word

"Please."

Alice was enraged.

"You are nothing but an animal," she screamed, bringing her hand across Kow's face in a heavy open handed slap.

"No," sobbed Kow, her voice like that of an unjustly scolded three-year-old. "I'm a girl. I'm just a girl like you."

There was something in the voice that for the first time ever reached Alice. It unsettled her. Kow was less than human, degenerate; whatever humanity she had once had, had died when she had been hit by the G-weapon.

This mutie was a source of spare parts that could save the sight of the thousands of radiation victims in the Radlands. She could be harvested for irises, lenses, retinal cells for implants, drained of the vitreous humour that she produced. It was a simple transaction of exploiting something that was not human for the benefit of humanity. But she could only rationalize that transaction provided she was able to block out Kow's humanity.

She steeled herself, and blocked out any seed of sympathy that might take root and grow. The expression in her eyes hardened and she moved in close to Kow again. She felt the blonde pubic hair of her victim lightly brushing against the back of her hand as she got ready to pluck another eye from her flesh.

Working quickly now she harvested the line of eyes, popping them one by one into the palm of her hand and then placing them on the surface of the little cart she had pulled into the cell with her. Kow was openly crying now. Great sobs racking her body, and as each eye was ripped from her leg she cried out. Every eye on her body was now wide, terrified expressions staring out from her breasts, from between her ribs, the palms of her hands, every joint on her body. Small eyes nestled in with normal sized, some in clusters, and some by themselves. Each one that had a tear duct now cried.

The blood was flowing freely in a stream down her thigh, pooling on the floor under one ankle, where it covered the row of tiny eyes that had grown like a foam of white blisters around the line of her sole.

Her fingers now dripping with blood, Alice moved up Kow's body. She ran her hands up either side of her ribcage, as if frisking, but more gentle and with the intimacy of invasion. The pretence was gone now, Alice's breath came short, and she breathed out heavily through her nose. As she reached around to check along Kow's spine she felt her breasts come into contact with those of the mutie. She could feel the pressure of her skin, warm and real, only separated by the material of her t-shirt.

Suddenly she could feel the softness of lips against her own. Soft, unlike any kiss she had ever known. Her hands behind Kow's back, she felt eyeballs under her fingers, the kiss soft, the furious passion rising within her; she curled her fingers into the claw of the predator she had become. Gouging into her back, Kow opened her mouth in a soundless scream, and Alice consumed that scream. She could feel the blood spurting over her hands and the eyeballs moving under her expert touch. This was unlike anything she had ever done. The power was taking her.

Breathless and bloody she moved back a step, wiping her mouth with her hand, leaving a silky red smear. Her hair had come a little loose.

"Well, I think that's enough for today," she said, the tremble in her voice impossible to disguise. Shaken, she took her little cart, and the eyes that she had stolen from Kow, and left the cell, forgetting to release the restraints. Kow was left hanging, pulled out wide and unable to move, blood still streaming from the newly emptied sockets. But she still had eyes enough left to cry another thousand tears.

"I shall be back again tomorrow," Alice called over her shoulder.

LIQUID SKIN

She would be walking down the street, the grey concrete of a normal day. She would look down, the pavement a muted and colourless paste of brick, spotted with bleached chewing gum and seagull droppings. She would be struck by how much the runnels between the square tiles looked like the gaps between the chunks on a bar of chocolate, and then she would hear the crack.

It always sounded like a rifle shot, like ice breaking beneath her feet. She could always feel the surface give a little first, as if it had not quite broken all the way through. Looking down, the pavement would be crazed, like a smashed car window, circular and web-like, and oozing stickily through the cracks, welling up as though from a slow wound, came the dark, deliberate blood.

Stepping away, shocked and bewildered, the crack would happen again under her feet, but this time she could not stop herself, and her foot would always go right through into the blood below, warm and wet .

Pulling herself free, dripping and nauseous, she takes another step…crack…and another…crack. The concrete world is giving way under her. The breathless terror mounts, and she is overwhelmed with inchoate, primeval panic. Suddenly she is running, the floor under her feet cracking and crunching like the icing on a cake, cracking like ice, crunching like snow.

In panic she looks over her shoulder as she runs, and she can see her foot prints as dark wounds on the skin of reality, as if the whole world was nothing but a thin crust of insubstantial bone, below which waits a vast and unquiet ocean of blood, heaving beneath the surface.

She tries to scream, but her voice is lost. She can't seem to make any noise. She can't remember how to speak. She is too terrified. It feels like a great weight on her chest, and no sound comes. From away in the distance she can hear a pathetic whistling, peeping sound, she can hear it as a panic stricken and breathless whisper; she can hear the tears in it, even though she is not crying.

As she runs, she looks down, and the blood makes pat pat pat noises like the splash of a shallow puddle, like a child in bright red boots, playing in the rain; the rain becomes blood, the sky is bleeding.

She can feel its weak tackiness every time she lifts a foot to take a step, as if the blood is trying to hold on to her, to pull her down.

And then she would wake, tears in her eyes and anger in her heart. The tears of terror, and the anger of frustration. These dreams had plagued her as long as she could remember. Doctor Eams, the expedition psycher, had told her that they were either a function of stress, or a symptom of demonic possession.

Beale Voynitch lay panting on her camp bed, and wondered how it was that Walput had managed to drag her out to this god forsaken rim-world. She was a cryptographer pressed into the service of paleoxenology. Left to her own devices she would never have left the Earth, but Nageon Walput, the expedition leader, had insisted on her, and her alone. And what Walput wanted, Walput always got.

She swung her legs over the side of her cot and caught a glint as the pale sunlight reflected off the edge of one of her skates.

She had pitched her tent near the shore of Crystal Lake, two days hard travel from the main dig site at Alorep. Walput had been right, the writing of the Fairlight culture was a puzzle that had grabbed her imagination straight away. There was meaning in the strangely swirling figures, but without knowing anything about the species that had made them, or the language they used, there was no way to derive that meaning.

Her obsessive compulsive nature had ensured she had been sucked into the puzzle so totally that she barely noticed she was working eighteen hour days, never taking a day off.

Frequency analysis showed that the script was in part a small selection of repeating patterns which resembled letters or perhaps syllables, and other signs that seemed to appear less often but looked to have some kind of modification on the following group of signs.

She had been on Fairlight for close to two years now, and Dr. Eams had ordered her to take some time out.

"Why not go out to Crystal Lake, do some skiing, or some sky-boarding? It will be a break for you."

Beale had just shaken her head; she was too busy to be ill. She could not afford the time off. She had finally made a breakthrough with the written script of the Fairlight culture.

The language had been used to write down thought, directly, and as such was independent of language. If she could find the key, she would be able to read it directly, read the minds of a lost race.

She already had fragments, but they didn't seem to make much sense. The massive complex at Alorep appeared to be some kind of penal colony, but the vast machine that underpinned the structure was described by an idea that seemed to suggest a fantasy engine.

She ate a slow breakfast, alone on a deserted world. Walput had supported the doctor, and practically forced her out of her office. She looked at the large tent behind her, and turned to survey the milky ice of the lake spread out before her. As she sipped her coffee, the silence of a world without birds made the cold seem like the exciting winters of her childhood. Being so alone made her feel... she struggled to find the right word, and then realised it was…naughty.

She picked up her skates and walked down to the edge of the lake. The scenery was spectacular. An open heath in the orange of bracken and the purple of sagebrush, low trees, a light dusting of snow in patches, and in the distance, gentle hills rising to blend in with a giant golden mountain.

She had called this louring peak Mount Warder. This place had been a prison, she knew that from the writing inscribed upon almost every surface that the Fairlight culture had made, but she could see no bars. And somehow the machine under the surface of the planet was supposed to make fantasy a reality, to make wishes come true.

She found a fallen log and put on her skates. She laced them tightly, watching her breath come out in a plume of vapour as she bent to reach her feet. Gingerly she manoeuvred out onto the ice. Her progress was ungraceful as she held onto the branches of the bushes that grew at the side of the lake.

She was not worried about the thickness of the ice, a planetography crew had been there the previous year. They had taken an ice core that was more than three kilometres deep.

The ice was so smooth, it felt like plastic under the blades of her skates. With an unsteady push she set off from the bank and headed out into the lake, the great tobacco coloured flanks of Mount Warder ahead of her; its snow covered peak gave it the clarity of a child's drawing of a mountain.

The sound of her skates over the ice cut into her thoughts. She let it become almost mesmeric. The surface was so smooth, it was like shark skin, and her skates left two perfect lines behind her, like razor-blades drawn across the milky flesh of a corpse.

Behind her, underneath and deep, something moved. In the cracks, flowing slowly as if released from slumber, the blood began to rise. As her skates sliced through the skin of the ice, clouds of diluted and watery blood bloomed under the surface. Complex as rose petals.

She skated on, unaware of the twin tracks of red that kept pace with her, marking her progress across the alien lake.

Fantasy was such an odd word, she thought, perhaps wish would be closer to the concept. "For your crimes against us we sentence you to having your wishes come true." She tried the words out loud, but still could not see that it would be any great threat.

Behind her the blood had spilled out across the surface of the lake, pooling where her skates had liberated it, and where it had not, it boiled below, in angry clouds of crimson. She leaned into a turn, and faced back the way she had come.

Curtains of red moved under the ice, rolling this way and that, like a caged animal looking for escape. She looked down at her feet, the ice was now a thin and clear layer, like a pane of glass, and - ravenous beneath her - an unfathomable welling of blood. She took a deep shocked breath and turned back. The rest of the lake was suddenly the same. She was surrounded.

Not wishes, she realised with dreadful clarity, not wishes, but dreams. The solitary woman stood, too terrified to move; every limb trembled and she was without strength. She knew that this dream would have no waking end.

The sound was like that of a rifle shot as the ice began to crack.

WHITE WATER

"I don't think we're in North Dakota any more," Henri remarked as he surveyed the view of the storm tossed sea from the time-flyer's window. The *Tempus Fugit* was out of sight of land now, skimming fast and low over deep black waters.

"On the contrary, my simple friend," Professor Von Nudgevinck replied without lifting his eyes from the controls. "That is exactly where we are. Or more precisely, North Dakota is what this place will be called in around twelve thousand eight hundred years from now."

Henri glanced over at the crusty old Europesian, giving his "What do you take me for?" look.

"Professor," he said seriously, "there are no seas in North Dakota." This was met by one of the uncomfortable silences that Henri had come to dread.

"Tell me again, Henri, what you did at university."

"I majored in Temporal Tourism studies."

"You were there on a surfing scholarship!" exploded the professor. "And if you had turned up to the occasional lecture, then you would know that this is Lake Agassiz, one of the largest bodies of fresh water that the planet has ever known."

Henri shrugged and turned back to enjoying the view. The Prof. was mostly a relaxed type but he could turn a bit snappy after a time-jump. Henri also knew that he would be his normal self again as soon as he got some coffee.

"So why'd they name it after a tennis player?" he asked.

"AgassIZ!" yelled the Prof. after another short and stunned silence. "It is called Lake AgassIZ. After Louis Agassiz. You know, the geologist?"

"Never heard of her," replied Henri.

The atmosphere in the cabin became a little strained for the next ten minutes or so, as the two sat in bad tempered silence.

"So Prof.," Henri eventually ventured, "I never did figure out what you hope to learn from this trip."

"I despair of you," was the rather short reply.

The professor currently seemed to be of the opinion that Henri had the I.Q. of a duvet but the young man shrugged it off internally. He had his own reasons for being with the time travelling archaeologist, and putting up with a few grumbles and insults was a small price to pay for what he would get out of it. That was going to be his own time tour company specialising in deep-time extreme sports.

"This is where it all began," announced the professor suddenly with a wave of his right arm that encompassed the mass of water below them.

"Where all what began?"

"Everything. Civilisation, technology, culture, everything. The great human adventure starts here."

Henri looked from horizon to horizon; nothing but black water as far as he could see.

The professor glanced at his companion and realised that a little more explanation was needed.

"What do you see, Henri?"

"Water. A whole lot of water."

"And if we were to jump forward eighteen months, what do you think you would see?"

"More water, perhaps the occasional fish."

"And you would be wrong. All of this will be gone in around one year." Casually the professor adjusted the controls, and the sleek shape of the *Tempus Fugit* gained altitude as she crossed the future border into Minnesota.

"This is a glacial boundary lake. It only exists because of a colossal layer of ice covering the north of the continent. That ice sheet is blocking off the ocean and there is nowhere for the water from all the rivers in this giant valley to run off to. The result is this inland sea, seven hundred miles long by two hundred miles wide.

"We are here today because a few hours ago, the ice melted, and a channel has formed. This lake is now doomed, and millions of cubic kilometres of fresh water are about to be dumped into the Atlantic, turning off the warming effects of the THC, the circulation of warm water.

"The whole world is about to get very cold and very dry, and your ancestors are going to have to get a whole lot smarter to survive the next century.

"And they do," he added, almost as an afterthought. "This event is the start of the Younger Dryas, and in the Near East this change in climate is directly responsible for developments in agricultural practice that lead to the ideas of storage of surplus. And when you have food surplus, you suddenly have the ability to pay people to do stuff other than food production, like sing songs, or make dresses, or become an army. The stuff of humanity as we know it.

"Everything that our culture is built on: the invention of the brick, writing, the wheel, even beer, sausage, and barbecues, are all about to be invented because, for the next hundred years, it is going to get very cold and very dry. And this, what is happening here today, this out-flowing of Lake Agassiz, is what starts it all off."

Henri had glazed over. Since hooking up with the Prof., they had been all over. One trip had been the eruption of Krakatoa in 1883, one of the most spectacular displays of fiery violence the world had seen, and where else would he ever get the chance to surf a one-hundred-and-twenty foot tsunami? It had been the greatest buzz ever, like riding the Wedge, the Pipeline and Jaws all at once. On his force-field protected board, he had stayed ahead of the wave for three hours.

On their last trip, Henri had become the first human to cross the Atlantic on a surfboard. In the last three years of time travel Henri had invented extreme sports beyond the imaginings of previous generations.

This trip, however, was beginning to look like a bust. Just the geek stuff, and nothing he could use for his list of temporal holiday locations for when he set up his own time-tour company.

Abruptly the engine note changed as The *Tempus Fugit* slowed to hover. Ahead of the time ship, a great wall of ice rose from the surface of the lake.

"The Laurentide Ice sheet," said the professor, an unmistakable note of awe in his voice.

"What we have always wanted to know was, did the ice sheet split and collapse, or did the lake form a channel under the ice."

The answer before them was suddenly obvious. In the wall of ice, a huge mouth to a tunnel could be seen, several miles wide. The waters of Lake Agassiz were pouring into the massive fissure in the ice with the furious violence that only the really big movement of water can manage.

"I'll get the probe ready," said the professor, rising from the pilot's seat and going aft.

"Probe?" said Henri.

"Yes, probe. Are you now deaf as well? The purpose of the trip is to map this ice channel with a force-field protected probe."

Henri had a sudden twist in the way he saw things.

"You are saying that this tunnel stretches all the way to the sea?"

"Yes, obviously, Henri."

"A huge tunnel, passing through cataracts and splits and caverns in the ice, eventually feeding out into the ocean?"

"Yes."

"And passing through it would be like some super combination of cave diving, white water rafting, and a trip on Space Mountain if it were a flume."

"I suppose you could look at it like that."

"I'll get my board," said Henri. Perhaps, he thought, this birth of civilisation thing might not be so dull after all.

MANGO DICTIONARY AND THE DRAGON QUEEN OF CONTRACT EVOLUTION

"Dragons." The Waylarn paused for effect. "Lots of them…all over the place."

The Lady Mango formed one eyebrow into a perfect arch as she listened.

"Interesting," she said. "And what exactly is it that you expect me to do about it?"

The Waylarn winced, visibly nerving himself up to his diplomatic task.

"When you were banished from Earth, it was always said that you were fiddling with sorcery."

"The word, Waylarn, is meddling, not fiddling." She fixed him with a gaze of razor sharp green steel. "Mango Dictionary does not "*fiddle*" with anything." The courtier winced again.

"I'm sorry, milady. I will keep that in mind."

"You would best be advised to do exactly that, Waylarn. The *Cantus Belli* may be an old ship, but she is an old *Earth* ship, and directly above this pathetic pig-farm you call a colony. Are you familiar with the saying, "Newbility needs no reason"?

"Yes, milady." The Waylarn lowered his gaze. "But Contract Evolution has become your own personal fiefdom. We pay you our tribute. We are your people, your thanes, can we not come to you with our grievances in time of need?"

The Lady Mango Stargazy in Illness Conceived under the Purple Skies of Magdalene Dictionary (the third) slowly realized that the pudgy, badly-dressed and sweaty individual in the coms field was doing what no other man in her entire life had ever done. He was standing up to her.

She lay back on her chez-tongue, momentarily admiring the courage of the man. He knew that the *Cantus Belli* was linked to her every whim. He must have been completely aware that the vast imperial relic that hung over his world had the power to swat him as if he was nothing but an insect, and yet, he still had the bravery to press his case.

"Very well, Waylarn, your pleas have moved me and I will investigate."

"Oh milady, th…"

His thanks ended abruptly as a large-bore blast-cannon tracked the com signal back to its point of origin and wiped the odious little commoner from the face of existence. The Lady Mango even allowed herself a wry and somewhat self-satisfied smile at the thought of all his brave little atoms now being wafted around the skies of the disgusting, and apparently dragon ridden, world of Contract Evolution.

However, she would investigate. Her word was as good as a sworn vow. The vast gothic gold hull of the *Cantus Belli* stretched like a waking cat. Statues sighed and corridors constricted. Energy fields fluxed and flexed as the old ship, called the Hammer of Freedom by the long defeated Republican Star Force of French Mars, felt the desires within the Lady Mango and reconfigured herself to be more suited to the Lady's whim.

Malleable metal morphed - mutating, melting and melding. Mango moved, the long train of her dress rustling as it flowed liquid and seamlessly into the organic marble deck. Sumptuous, gold and black, the extruded material that flowed from the old ship swirled around the Lady like the surging coastal sea-foam thrown against the ebon rocks of her birthworld. The *Cantus Belli* clothed her with itself, and in return the Lady Mango became the heart of the island in the sky.

They had been joined at the soul since Mango had reached puberty. The *Cantus Belli* had accepted her as its own flesh, and the Lady Mango had become the soul of the leviathan. The conjoining of the two had been destined since the genetic compatibility of her parents had been calculated from across all the great houses of the Empire, and the Emperor himself had consented to be her cousin.

That had all been before the fall.

Mango began to descend, a bubble of decking forming around her as the *Cantus Belli* lowered her gently through the structure of the ship. She was transported like a morsel trapped in the vacuole of an amoeba, until with a sigh, the *Cantus Belli* lovingly opened up the rooms of the shuttle collection.

Drifting between pillars of gold, torches burning in recesses, Mango laid herself on a viewing throne and the *Cantus Belli* wafted shuttles before her until she spotted one that suited her mood.

A sphere of flowing information crystallised, becoming solid around her, and she became entwined with its fabric. Mango Dictionary and the *Cantus Belli* became almost distinct and separate. The shuttle was kissed into space, a bubble that contained all that mattered in the universe to the relic of times long forgotten.

The Lady Mango stood as if on a magic carpet, in her left hand a single crystal ball, the perfect sphere of Contract Evolution filling her vision as she left the imperial leviathan behind.

The planet before her was mud brown from pole to pole, and the reason for the mud brown colour was that Contract Evolution was a sea of mud from pole to pole. The *Cantus Belli* could not completely explain the roundness of Contract Evolution but the Lady Mango had been satisfied with a "best guess", which was that at some point in the fledgling planet's history a near miss with another object had melted the entire surface, and Contract Evolution had become the roundest and nearest to spherical planet ever discovered by the spreading rash that was humanity.

Contract Evolution had no basins and no depths but it did have a lot of water, which covered the entire surface of the world to a depth of a few inches. As Mango floated downwards, descending like a vampire on a virgin neck, she was again struck by the perfect complexion of this world. It swirled like an opal with shades of brown, the perfect white clouds marbling the marble; a world that looked like a cake, or a perfect smooth gem.

Mango scanned the world with her gaze, looking for anything that might resemble a permanent way-mark. But there was nothing. The colonies were simple rafted affairs drifting over the placid mud-sea of Contract Evolution, straining the planet-covering soup for whatever could be sold on the interstellar auction sites.

The Lady Mango penetrated the atmosphere, her crystal sphere of a magic carpet now a projectile that seared the sky as a bullet of pure flame. The expression on her face was as serene as her heart, which saw the approaching world with nothing but a slight sharpening of appetite.

The shuttle was filled with the music of angels chanting over the pits of hell and the demons below responding. Chiming and dramatic, she fell on Contract Evolution, looking for a dragon, or some dragons, or even lots of dragons. But what she really wanted to find was an explanation.

The Waylarn's image had originated near the North Swirl, the part of the planet where the mud of the surface swirled like the locks of Mango's perfect crown.

She stared into the crystal ball that she held and mapped the planet below. The eyes of the old ship above her roved the surface looking for the tell-tale signs of living beings, and the *Cantus Belli* found them, in their thousands scattered all across the world. Yet not one was anything other than those species that humanity had carried between the stars.

Had the Waylarn sacrificed his life for a joke? The Lady Mango's perfect eyes changed to a deep violet, cat's iris's to match her tiger mood. If this was some attempt to fool her, then she had the claws to make sure that no such cancer could take root within her fiefdom.

The crystal surface of the shuttle faded as to be invisible and Mango flew above the planet-wide sea. She stood regal but ready to strike. Her desire before it reached thought was enough to steer her course. This was what her life had always been like; before she knew that she wanted something, it had already been provided. That had been what had led to her downfall and why she and the *Cantus Belli* now skulked in the outer fringes of the poorer sections of the empire.

Her fury surged around inside her, a roiling ocean of brimstone that would not let her rest. The resentment of her cousin and those courtiers that had consigned her to the outer darkness burned in her heart, a magma core of revenge looking for a weak spot to erupt and blast away at all that had confined her.

Her eyes scanned the surface of the world. "Dragons, lots of them, all over the place". That was what he had said, and she had made the trip to find them, and there were no dragons, and she had already dealt with the Waylarn. Well, she would have to find someone else to punish for this deception, she thought.

The surface of the mud below began to stir. Ripples and rivulets gave the uniform brown the appearance of having been combed. Then a hump began to form down the centre of the disturbance. Mango was now a mere twenty metres from the world, and the disturbed area stretched as far as her unaided eye could see.

The brown mud now had a current. Mango followed the flow. A gradient was beginning to form and the current became a torrent, brown water cascading down a sudden hill. Then, from the mud, Mango could see the ripples of muscle, spines erupting in a kilometre long row ahead of her. She climbed into the sky to get a better look at what was happening around her.

She was unused to fear, unknown to it and it to her. The *Cantus Belli*, her immortal and all powerful lover and ally, was there as a shield; an impenetrable armour through which not even the awareness of a danger could pass. So it was that when she realised what she was witnessing was the birth of a dragon of geological scale, ripping itself from the very fabric of the world below, she was charting unknown emotional territory.

Bowel loosening in size, the great drake spread her wings. Mango could see flight muscles dragging the membranous sails free of the mud-ocean.

The Lady Mango now stood braced against the back wall of her shuttle sphere, her arms spread out wide, and she wondered what the sound that she could hear was before realising   it was her own panting. Colour flashed across the leathery skin of the dragon, flashing iridescent scales taking on the patterns of butterflies' wings. She shimmered like oily water and rainbow skies, and tens of kilometres away the neck began to rise up, long and slender and strong, roped and laced with sinew and more powerful than the attraction of distant atoms.

Set atop the pillar of dragon flesh, Mango realised that she was looking at the back of the freshly born dragon's head. Great scaled horns rose above the brow and pointed ears pricked with obvious alert and vicious intelligence.

Mango stood on her magic carpet feeling completely exposed to the might of this sudden change in the universe. Microscopic, an insect to be flicked in to oblivion without consideration or consequence.

Then, as if hearing a sound behind her, the great dragon twisted her head on that gigantic tower of a neck and Mango found herself under the scrutiny of a vast wheel of a bejewelled eye.

Above her the *Cantus Belli* could feel the depth and urgency of her fear, yet those ancient eyes, built at the beginning of human civilisation and never bettered, could see nothing. Mango screamed, and the *Cantus Belli* shuddered at the sound. Weapons formed on the planetward surface of the ancient vessel, erupting bolts of energy and fury. The sky around the Lady Mango burned with a hard rain of the Earth's imperial rage. Cannonade and twisting pillars of energy criss-crossed the back of the dragon behemoth. The lady looked into the dragon's eyes and saw that the vast beast was laughing at her. Laughing at Mango Dictionary.

The dragon turned. Contract Evolution shook and quaked under the strain of supporting the queen of all dragons. She clawed the globe, and with a supersonic flick of wings and tail, she faced the Lady Mango. The dragon queen rose up on her haunches, wrapping her tail around herself as if it were a snake and spreading her wings so as to block out the sky. And then the dragon took a breath.

Mango knew about dragons, humans carried dragons with them in their genes. It had always been as if somehow humans were aware of the Great Drakes through some thin curtain of reality. As if they were always next door, separated from us by nothing more substantial than flimsy gauze. Mango knew that the dragon summoned gale that filled the lungs of the beast would erupt again in a tsunami of flame, a tempest of fire, the fury of the dragon made fierily manifest. She also knew, without even a hint of doubt, that the shuttle and all the might of the *Cantus Belli* would not, could not protect her from the rage of this ruthless draconian queen.

With a smile of malicious intent, the dragon began to swoop down on the Lady Mango. Mango heard herself scream, the music still playing in her shuttle, and her scream, ripped from a part of her soul she had never known, was a perfect high note and fitted to her symphony of terror as if written to it.

Black smoke escaped the fumaroles of the dragon's nostrils, forced aside by the dragon swoop as the Queen came for the Lady.

Finally the Lady Mango crystallised her desire to be elsewhere and the shuttle began to climb into the heavens. She ran away. Never before, not even in her dreams, had she had need to flee, but now she knew the desire to run. She felt its power and she gave into it. The shuttle shot into the deep-dark of the sky like a tear of crystallized, burning, whimpering dread. Behind her the dragon leapt into the heavens. Great leathery sails of wings, each one the size of a continent, flapped twice, releasing tornadoes across the brown sea. The tornadoes became waterspouts, vertical twisting walls of water, towering above the flimsy rafts of the colonists.

Mango looked over her shoulder, her open mouthed and breathless terror coalescing as a fist of unshakable pain in her chest. The jaws of the dragon mother stretched wide, each tooth the size of a mountain.

Then, with a feeling as if the whole universe was laughing at her, Mango's eyes saw but could not comprehend that the dragon queen was disintegrating into a flock of thousands of cackling dragonoras, then each dragonora split into hundreds of dragons of all colours and temperatures. The dragons split into iridescent dragonettes, and then the dragonettes into a rainbow of draglet drops, and finally the cloud of draglets faded from view like a subsiding chuckle.

Mango looked towards the dark. The *Cantus Belli* filled the whole of the sky above as it rushed to gather her up. With the urgency of a mother sweeping up a fleeing child, the shuttle was absorbed into the fabric of the great ship. Mango, shaken and shocked, slumped - sliding slowly she subsided, still sobbing, struggling to understand the scale of what she had seen. The wreck of the Lady was carried through the halls of the ship to her throne room. The *Cantus Belli* held her safe, and without knowing that she had wanted it, the old Earth ship kicked away from the gravity well of Contract Evolution and headed into the deep-dark.

Far below, on the surface of the Contract Evolution and half a world away from the site of his apparent demise, the Waylarn smiled as he disconnected from the device. It was ancient, and no one could say whether it was alien or human made, but it could summon up a fair old dragon when it wanted to.

IT'S A TEMPLE

IT'S A TEMPLE

IT'S A TEMPLE

IT'S A TEMPLE

IT'S A TEMPLE

For the Attention of Prof Dolly Roxette
Professor of Pre-Federal Studies, Angel Cody Institute,
University of Sangelese.

Serra Pedagogica bich,

Introductio, Nathan Cody-Smith. Editorio Sangeles Journal of Imaginative Archaeology. Ina inglisi dansa Sangelese publicatea ab 103FR.

Traveyoi ina "Tales from B4" Vidio, en per…..nd was impressed not just by the obvious scholarship, but also by the quality of the storytelling. From what I saw, you have a gift for a phrase.

Whilst not peer reviewed, The Sangelese Journal of Imaginative Archaeology has become the foremost archaeological digest of the inner system, and has a circulation that now stretches to the most distant outworlds. The further that humanity travels from home, the greater is its desire to know about the place where we all came from.

To that end I would like to invite you to submit a piece on your specialised area of the late pre-federal period. What I'm looking for is a vignette, perhaps a dramatisation that creates a picture of what it would have been like to live before the Time of Troubles. A snapshot of a decadent culture at its height.

I look forward to your reply.

Steamy Loving,
Nathan Cody-Smith, Editor

FAO Nathan Cody-Smith, Editor
Sangelese Journal of Imaginative Archaeology
13[b] Street of Shame, Canton of Clan Smith
Sangelese

Most Esteemed Editor Fellow,

As a professor of pre-federal history, and a field archaeologist with the University of Sangelese, the period immediately prior to the war, stretching from about 90B4 up until first contact with the iL'Kizz, is for me, without a doubt, the most fascinating of all human eras. It was a time of technological sophistication, coupled with fearsome naivety. Even the most cursory tour of the Broken Cities makes such a conclusion tragically obvious.

I received your request for a contribution to your august organ with a certain amount of trepidation. I am often asked to provide a layman's picture of what life in the latter days of the land of La might have been like, and I think we have now reconstructed and retrieved enough to create a reasonable image of the whole.

"Buster's Big Day Out" is my attempt to catch the ethos of an average day for an average inhabitant of La in about 73B4. I have included full annotated footnotes for the more academic of your readership, but should also caution that subscribers of a delicate disposition may be shocked by the barbaric practises that our ancestors considered as everyday and commonplace.

It was my intention to create both a compelling narrative and a historically accurate picture, and hope that the academic correctness of the piece does not overpower the story. Your comments on this point would be appreciated.

With Hot Love,
Dolly Roxette,
Professor of Pre-Federal Studies, Angel Cody Institute,
University of Sangelese

Buster's Big Day Out
A Speculative Fabulation by Prof Dolly Roxette

Buster lifted his gaze from his Personal Computulator, heaved himself with some effort from the couch, and walked over to the televizualisor, or Telly V, as it was also known. This was the spring of 73B4 and "I Love Lucy" was having its first run. Buster turned the noise up.

In common with most of his compatriots at the time, he found the irritating voice of the famous redhead hysterically funny. Life was simple then, and the ill-fated United States of America was a young country with a population that had been drawn from many different ethnic, linguistic, and cultural backgrounds. It was a time that only unsophisticated things could become successful, because of the need to be transcultural in appeal.

Buster's room was L-shaped, and covered with a thin layer of woven material which had been gathered from the back of a domesticated ruminant.[1] He hardly noticed its rough texture at all, as he had two pieces of hardened dried animal skin strapped to his feet for protection.

Reluctantly he turned the huge knob on the front of the Telly V, stopping the electricity that coursed down the wires lining the walls of his dwelling. The Telly V issued a huge mechanical "clunk" and the great glass valves cooled. The laughter that accompanied the deliberately moronic tellyplay faded to silence.

It was time for Buster to "go out".

He went upstairs to his room to put on his outside clothing. Atmospheric corrosives were unknown in those days, so keeping warm and dry were his only concerns.

It was a happy age, those last few years before the war, and everywhere, in everything, colours were bright and garish. Buster chose a garment of hooped corduroy in bright green and vivid blue[2]. To compliment the effect he topped the outfit off with a blouse, or chemise, of yellow "silk" (a material derived from boiled insect carcasses.)[3]

He was ready to leave now. He picked up his juju trinkets, a small collection of almost bladelike metallic pieces that were all threaded together onto a shiny steel ring. He raised it to his lips and kissed the blessed items, one by one. It was widely believed by all his friends and family that such juju trinkets would ward off the evil spirits that the new machines were bringing to the world. President James Kennedy, the leader of the United States of America, the country that Buster lived in, had

---

1   See Harris and Beccles "Carpet: The Final Mystery" New Vegas University Press, FR150, pp138
2   A reconstruction of the Sausalito Pantaloon is on permanent display at the Unity Museum of Human History in Sangelese
3   See "Sericulture: A Guide for the Squeamish" Frossette and McNeal, Ancorp Academic Publishing 189 FR

recently been killed riding in the back of such a machine[4].

He left the house by its front entrance and with his head bowed. He shuffled as if in a religious procession, around the side of the building and went into the attached temple. This was the place where he stalled his sacred mechanism.

It was with some trepidation and a great deal of reverence that Buster approached this machine, a conveyance called an autocar. A simple wheeled affair powered by exploding hydrocarbons, the autocar had become the ubiquitous expression of the religion of the culture.

Automotivism was, before the Time of Troubles, a worldwide cult. The remains of Autocars are found wherever there are human settlements, and are the major type-fossil of the age. His own autocar was a fearsomely powerful vehicle called a Jord and it was capable of velocitude in excess of eighty kilometres per hour over the ground.

After his house, the autocar was the biggest thing in Buster's life, it was his pride and joy,[5] and he gained much kudos in his peer group from its conspicuous expense. To pilot an autocar was called driving, so Buster drived his autocar from its temple, onto the metal of the road, and by dexterous use of his feet he made it go to its max fastness. The sky was a dazzling and irrational blue, without even the slightest hint of yellow, and the clouds were sparse and high. He told the car that he wanted it to drive by the ocean.

Buster lived on the outskirts of an unimaginably vast settlement called East La, and the tragedy that loomed over the great cities of the west was still far beyond the horizon. He was heading north to meet his woman friend. She was a popular entertainer of the day called Madonna.[6] They were off to Hollywood to see a pictures called Star Wars, but before that, they had arranged to meet and have a ritual meal together in one of the many popular eating establishments that had sprung up to take advantage of the abundance of cheap food on the America continent.

Buster pulled into the burgering and went inside the gaily painted eating-place. Doris was waiting for him at one of the many small round tables.

The burgering made and sold a flat pancake called patty. Patty was made from reconstituted flesh of eviscerated domestic animals, although probably not cats or dogs…

---

4   On nearly every skeleton excavated from within the broken cities, one of these small rings of metallic amulets has been found. Their use was obviously ritual. For a discussion of the ubiquitous juju trinket phenomenon and its cult see Winter Twist et al. "Spirit Charms of the Pre-Federal Era" New Moon Publishing, New Moon 4, 186FR
5   Status in the pre-federal era was based on possession and income rather than more valuable cultural and scientific attainment, a situation that would eventually be perceived as one of the root causes of "Dumbing Down" and indirectly of CivWar II. See "Morons with Money: Death of a culture" Dino Velasquez's seminal work.
6   The real name of the singer known as Madonna is an area of contention but this author thinks that the most likely candidate is probably Doris Day, although compelling cases have also been made for, amongst others, Louise Armstrong and Gladys Schwarzenegger

Serra bich …

I'm sorry but I'm going to have to pass on "Buster's Big Day Out", Professor Lady, but I seem to have given you the wrong impression of exactly what it was that I was after. I enclose a copy of the Journal, as you seem not to have taken into account the house style of the publication.

Essentially the Buster narrative is a little too dry for our readership. We are catering for a society of humans that span light-years. The purpose of our magazine is to remind the isolated population what it means to be civilised, to be part of humanity. The lone terraforming specialist, two years from the nearest civilised system, could not care less about Buster's hooped corduroy pants, or his meat eating habits, or even his argument with his girlfriend. (The choice of Madonna was probably not a wise one btw, as it is common knowledge that she was a fictitious character like Sherlock Holmes or Dorothy Lamore).

What the readers of the Sangelese Journal of Imaginative Archaeology want is the juice, the scurrilous details of a culture based on personal indulgence. We live in a time of widespread privation, and the wild history of the pre-federal era is an escape fantasy.

From the deepie camps of the Indiana radlands to the scumling communities of New Moon 4, a few minutes reading about the fleshpots of the last century B4 can take a trapped soul out of their own existence, and let them into a world where they can daydream about wealth and safety.

You know this period better than anyone else in Sangelese, and I have read your work in other publications. So it is with regret that I pass on Buster. Please do not regard this as a rejection, as we would very much like a piece from you, but it just needs to be more in line with the spirit of our publication.

Hot Love,
Nati

Most Esteemed Editor Fella,

I have now had a chance to peruse your sad excuse for a magazine, and find it to be an extruded piece of filth of the worst kind. I feel absolutely no shame in the fact that Buster was rejected, and I'm staggered that the likes of Prof Toklis and Dr Twist have allowed themselves to become prostituted into providing the soft-core pornographic stories that appeared in the issue that you sent me.

As for the graphical representations that accompanied the stories, well, no wonder your "*Journal*" is popular with the lonely of the galaxy.

I shall in future limit myself to academic publishing, safe in the knowledge that my ideas and my words are not heading out to sully minds across all of inhabited space. You might as well have sections like Orgies of the Ottomans, or the Revels of Rome.

I consider myself to be a well-adjusted member of Ancorp corporate culture and not easily shocked, but the trivialisation of the destruction of our last high civilisation, and the pornographication of anything remotely serious in order to sell more units, is a symptom of the decadence of our own society.

You are part of that "bottom line", a concept that cheapens us as a species, and as a society. I will have nothing more to do with you.

Peace on you,

Prof Roxette

Serra Bich,

It is with great regret that I read your previous communication (although your idea about the history of revels and orgies is definitely worth following up), and whilst I understand that an academic of your standing would be loath to contribute to a populist platform such as this one, I feel it would not be unfair to point out that we have already had contributions from some of the leaders in all the main fields of current archaeological work, including Prof Narbandian, head of the Ancorp Institute of Paleoxenology, and Prof van Broekinhetwaterland, chief of the Unity Emergency Xenolinguistics Squad.

Prof van Broekinhetwaterland allowed us to use a very seductive image of herself at the masthead of her piece "the Tongues of Teshub", and since that article appeared she has gone on to be nominated for the Tanhauser Prize. So it is with confidence that I can assure you that an association with the Sangelese Journal of Imaginative Archaeology is in no way detrimental to you academic career.

Hot Love,
Nati

Slime in Chief,

I have no idea why you continue to communicate with me. I would have thought
that I had made both my position and my disgust perfectly plain. I'm only sending this
because there is one point in your last diarrheic outpouring of verbiage that needs to
be countered.

To me it would matter not one jot if Kharis Pwall himself were to come down
from New Moon 4 and contribute to your magazine; it would not affect my opinion
of you, only of him. So you can take all your Toklis's, Twists and benighted Broekin-
hetwaterlands, and crawl back under whatever rock you emerged from, and I hope
that you're all very happy together

Peace and Love,

Prof Roxette.

Serra Bich,

The sharpness of your tongue is very definitely a marketable commodity, and
also strangely exciting. Did I mention that the Journal pays 500 Kilobills for every
published article?

Hot Love,

Nati

Licentious in Lycra – Sensuous in Spandex

Prof Dolly Roxette explores the sensual world of Pre-federal fibres and materials.

A scratch and sniff series in ten parts

Part one: Leather and Rubber, their uses in the recreation dungeons of the last
century B4.

DON'T SPOIL THE PARTY

Andy Bell raised the brandy balloon he was holding towards the computer screen and made a silent vow. He would, he decided, dedicate the remaining years of his life purely to the pursuit of meaningless sex, unnecessary risk and endless partying.

He stood, a skinny man, in a loose fitting and shabby T-shirt with a logo that had been funny in the nineteen-eighties, his thinning hair overlong and straggly. Still holding his brandy, he saw the middle-aged travesty of his younger self reflected in the black glass of his study window, and realised that it might not be such an easy vow to keep.

For twenty years the whole focus of his life had been turned outwards, away from the domestic and towards extra-solar planets. He worked on planetary formation models that could explain the vast gas-giants found in close orbits to these distant stars.

All the maths he had ever seen pointed to their forming in the outer system, acting as cold sweepers. He toyed with the idea of migration but never really found a convincing mechanism to explain it.

Eventually his career moved on, and he became involved in a project to map the Inter Stellar Medium, the Loop I super bubble, topological mapping of the Heliosphere - the local fluff. All nuts and bolts stuff, but then the data started coming in from the two Voyager probes as they hit the Heliosheath.

Voyager-two had reached the heliopause a couple of years earlier than expected. The conclusion was obvious. The shape of the bow-wave of particles the sun pushes before it was being distorted.

Andy began modelling from the data and eventually realised that the dent in the heliopause was the bow-wave of another object approaching the sun. He had calculated the mass of the object, and position, correlated it with observations, and realised that there was no detectable object at the place he expected.

He remembered the sickening plunge his stomach had taken when he realised that if there was no detectable object, there might be an undetectable one.

He tried to convince himself that he was suffering from stress. Obsessive compulsive disorder was making him paranoid. He spent days trying not to think about it, but the worry was like a cancer eating at him. He had to know. He had to find out. Was a black hole about to stray through the solar system?

At first he thought that the obvious answer was "no". Nothing escapes from a black hole, so if one was approaching, the heliopause would be pulled towards it, not repelled. He was reassured for a few days, until he started to think that if the black hole were already in the system, the sun's bow-wave would be pulled in behind it, causing a distortion that was not announcing its coming but marked the path it had already taken.

The shape and size of the distortion, factored against the outward rush of the solar wind, gave him the size and vector of the object.

He worked out a preliminary track for what he now was convinced was a small black hole, and was relieved to find that at its closest approach it would come no closer than the orbit of Jupiter. He had gone out and quietly celebrated, going to a local bar and shooting a few frames of pool. It was just as he was watching his opponent pocket the eight-ball for the fifth time that evening, he realised that he had only calculated for distance. He raced back to his machine and worked out the orbital calculations. The black hole would pass through the orbit of Jupiter, but where would the planet be?

The track missed, there would be no collision, but Andy's relief was short lived as he watched the simulated black hole pass behind the simulated gas giant. What he saw next made him reach for the brandy. For the duration of the pass, the mass of the black hole behind the orbit of the planet exerted its full attraction on Jupiter. Not enough to drag it in, but enough to slow its orbital velocity.

Andy worked out the effects of an object the size of Jupiter with a reduced orbital velocity, no longer enough to fight off the pull of the sun. Jupiter would inevitable spiral inwards, until it found the new point that mass and velocity would keep it falling around the sun. Andy realized that he finally had his mechanism for the migration of gas giants into close solar orbit.

Over the weeks he refined his simulation, until on his screen he could see the mighty juggernaut of Jupiter swinging up behind, and eventually catching the pea-sized Earth, either hurling it into the sun, or the eternal darkness of deep space.

He thought about publishing, announcing his findings, but asked himself what would be the point? These were forces of a scale beyond humanity's ability to deal with them. In a matter of a few tens of years the Earth was doomed, and so was all life on her. Nothing could be done. It seemed a shame to put such a downer on people.

"Don't spoil the party," he told his reflection in the study window. "Eat drink and be merry." He raised his glass to toast himself. "For tomorrow we die," he said, deciding to get a hair cut.

THE REVENGE OF SCHRÖDINGER'S CAT

Daniel Baker: Authorized mail
Trans-Chicago PTT
Return: Tinker05@TC.orb

Hi Pip,

Your mom tells me I need to explain to you exactly why I missed your birthday. I know I promised to be there, but sometimes we can't always do the things we want to. The truth is I'm in the brig for disorderly conduct, which is why I couldn't send a facemail. I don't know if you know what the brig is, you're growing up so fast and I'm missing so much of it; it's like jail but on a ship or in my case spaceship.

I'll be out in a couple of days, and I'll be on the first elevator capsule back down to Earth, but let me explain why I'm stuck here now. It's all about my cat, Tinker.

For the last two months I've had to share my cabin with a cat-hating satellite rigger called Barney Greenhurst. He's always calling my Tinker a stupid mog. (You met Tinker last time you came to stay, the bad tempered little tabby cat that wouldn't move off the ceiling the entire time you were in the cabin).

I remember the first time I saw him; I still had my place to myself then, before the contractors moved in. I was strapped into my zero-gravity bunk trying to read, when this protesting furry bullet flew past, facing backwards and mewling pathetically, his little tail spinning like a cartoon propeller.

One of the feral cats in the bilges had had kittens and Tinker, adventurous from birth, didn't master zero-gravity straight off. He must have slipped away from his mother and got caught up in the ventilation system, which promptly spat him out into my cabin.

I reckon he was about ten weeks old. I was missing you and your mother very much at the time (I still do and always will as long as my job takes me into space), but this unexpected bit of feline company livened up my life no end, particularly when he took to sharpening his claws on the lining of my spacesuit. That was a habit that led to my having an extra-specially lively day. I now keep his claws well and truly clipped.

However, when Barney moved in, the fact that I had a cat became a source of some friction between us. I have often met people who seem to have a deep dislike of cats, but this was the first time I had to share my living space with one. Things kept getting worse between us until one day last week I passed Eddie Fairlight's daughter, Amber, on the way down to the orbital elevator. She told me that Barney was conducting a real life test of Erwin Schrödinger's famous experiment, and broadcasting it out city-wide on the Trans-Chicago public access broadcast system.

Now, I need to know about Schrödinger's Cat because of my job. It was a thought experiment suggested by the father of quantum mechanics; although I've always felt that it teaches us more about the mind of Erwin Schrödinger than it does about the way that the universe behaves.

Simply put, Pip, it runs like this. A cat is put into a box, with a device for detecting particle decay, and a small bottle of poison, and then sealed so that no outside observer can have any information on the state of the cat/detector/poison system. If the detector senses atomic decay, the bottle of poison is smashed, and the cat dies.

The important bit is that Schrödinger then asked the question "is the cat in the box alive or dead?" to which he supplied the answer, "neither. It is in a state of flux." Reality inside the box is separated from reality outside, so the cat fades into a sort of magical mist called a superposition, where it's not really alive or properly dead. If anyone then opens the box the universe rushes in and makes one of the possibilities into reality. The big idea is that if you look at something it changes what's being looked at.

Now, as I said, I have to understand that for my job, but the important thing for you to hold on to, Pip, is the words "thought experiment". Which is a nice way of saying "think about what would happen if…"

Schrödinger never did it for real. He wasn't even thinking about cats anyway, the experiment was about sub-atomic particles. However, when I heard that Barney *was* doing it for real I knew it was nothing to do with sub-atomic particles, and I also knew straight away where he had found the cat.

I flew through the corridors. My Tink needed rescuing and nothing was going to get in my way. I've been living in zero-G for the last seven years now, and when I want to get across town quickly, well let's just say that Superman has nothing on me. I know every no-G handle, every kick-plate, trampet and swivel-pole between the docks and the city-bridge. I must have been doing about sixty when I barged through the door of the studio. I've seen the recording a few times now; the look on Barney's face!

He was talking into a floating camera and before him was a box. He took one look at my expression and obviously decided that the joke had gone far enough.

"It's only blue paint," he shouted as he backed away. I ignored him. I had more important things to do. I approached the box. My Tink was inside, according to Schrödinger he was now in a state of flux, and that only by opening the box would I make one possibility become reality. At least I now knew that the choice was between blue and not blue.

Carefully I removed the lid, and there was my Tink, front paws folded, sitting like a little sphinx, blinking in the sudden light. I looked him up and down to make sure he was uninjured, and started to laugh. I had always thought that Schrödinger's cat was a rubbish experiment, but Tink had managed accidentally to jam his tail between the hammer and the glass container of blue paint that Barney had put together. He really was in a state of flux, neither blue, nor not blue.

As he realized that he was free he kicked away from the box. I have been around G-less cats long enough to realize that they get around by jumping, so I managed to catch him, and in the same movement stuff him into the front of my jacket.

Where his tail had been jammed in the mechanism, the box started at first to go with him, but as Tinker kicked, the box came free. Spinning gently through the zero-g, almost in slow motion, it landed on Barney's head. There was a slight "poof" sound of a compressed air explosion.

The monitors gave each of us a week in the brig for disorderly conduct, but Barney is being transferred dirt-side, so I get my cabin back, and because he used indelible paint he'll be a rather fetching shade of blue for about the next six months. Schrödinger's cat, in the form of Tinker, finally gets his revenge.

Doctor Eams said he would look after Tink for me, and I have a little vacation owing to me, so what you get for your birthday, my dear Pip, will be the biggest hug a father ever gave, and probably a week in Potterland just to let you know exactly how sorry I really am.

Lots of love and I'll see you in a couple of days.

Your jailbird dad.

FROG IN A BUCKET

"I'm not a real frog," said the frog.

Space Corps' founder and most celebrated explorer, Horatio Strovic tapped his atmospheric o-meter. He was expecting hallucinations, but not this early in the process.

"I'm not going to talk to a 'not real frog'," he said, "even if it does pass the time before the air runs out."

"Would you honestly prefer me to be an all croaking, fly-swallowing, living frog?" said the frog, sounding aggrieved. "You wouldn't get much of a conversation out of it, trust me I know."

"Look," said Strovic, unaccountably exasperated at having to explain the nature of his own delusion to a delusion of his own. "You are merely a straight forward hallucination from the chemical build-up in my brain resulting from my air-scrubber having been sabotaged."

"Have it your own way, Captain." And with that the frog said nothing further.

Strovic sort of expected the little apparition to vanish, but it persisted, sitting on his main drive display, little froggy fingers resting on the coolant purge icon.

"Could you move over a bit, you're making me nervous sitting just there."

"Captain, you have done remarkably well." The frog had obviously decided to try again. "Your ship is travelling at above ninety percent of the speed of light, and because you're in a Magueijo fast-track, you relativistic speed is actually one hundred and three percent of C." The frog sat back on his haunches and clapped his hands together in a little round of applause. "Congratulations Captain, you are the first human to break the light barrier."

It was true, Strovic's vessel, the *Light Ship Highway*, was technically travelling faster than light. She powered through a naturally occurring corridor of space where the speed of light was slightly different to the rest of the universe; fossilized space-time from a period where C had a higher value.

"Strictly speaking," said the frog, "we think that you've cheated. Your understanding of the universe is based on the fallacy of relativity. You believe one of the most basic truths in the universe to be impossible. Yet you still managed to hurl yourself into the void above the speed of light. Our laws state that you are now by definition civilized. Personally I think you fluked it."

"Well, thank you very much. Nice to be appreciated. I take it that you are the galactic welcoming committee. I don't suppose you brought a new set of silver filters with you by any chance?"

"Sarcasm doesn't suit you, captain," said the frog. "And I'm not from your galaxy, and we are separated by about a billion and a half years, but otherwise spot on."

Strovic looked closer at the little frog. It looked exactly like a tree-frog, the sort that lives in bromeliads, but there was a hint of something sharp and intelligent in its bright red eyes. Hesitantly he reached out and gently prodded the creature. His fingers registered cold leathery skin, something like a congealed jelly.

"Why am I seeing a frog?" he asked

"It's really very simple," said the frog. "The universe is spinning. Does that give you a clue?"

"The universe is not spinning," said Strovic. "And I refuse to believe it is just because a frog tells me so."

"Please yourself, but the truth is that the universe is a finite physical structure made up as a super-fluid condensate. It has a physical boundary and a finite distance from edge to edge. The universe and the space-time condensate is entirely contained within what you charmingly refer to as a "black hole". Extra universal space is to all intents and purposes infinite, so your whole universe is a finite subset of an infinite dataset."

Strovic blinked once.

"Tell me about Zeno, Captain Strovic."

"Zeno? The philosopher?"

"Yes captain, the man that almost broke the light barrier when your world was wearing togas."

"You're the frog in the pond?"

"Ah," said the frog, "light dawns."

"A frog in a pond swims towards the edge of the pond, but he first has to cover half of the distance, and then half of the remaining distance, and then half that distance and so on ad infinitum. But it's a paradox because the frog eventually does get to the edge."

"Doesn't that give you a clue about the nature of space?" The frog sounded a little exasperated. Strovic answered him with a blank shrug.

"Travelling across a finite distance there will always be a remainder left over, so therefore it is not possible to cover a finite distance."

"But we live in a space where this does not apply. Converging wotsits, and the Greeks not having a word for zero and all that."

"Hmmm, that sounds likely, doesn't it?"

"Work it out, Horatio, you can do it. It's impossible to cross a finite distance. The universe is a finite physical structure set in a non-finite space. Come on, Captain, make the leap."

"So what you're saying is that all distances within the universe are a finite fraction of an infinite whole, and that a finite number divided by transfinite number is equal to zero, so therefore all distances must be equal to zero. The whole universe exists within a singularity?"

The frog slapped one of his little hands over his face in a gesture of total exasperation.

"Well I suppose you've got time to work it out," he said.

"If you hadn't noticed," said Strovic a little more sharply than he intended, "I'll be dead in two hours time, sabotaged by the Orbital separatists."

"Oh, didn't I mention?" said the frog innocently. "We've been on the lawn of the Whitehouse for the last five minutes. If you want a breath of fresh air, all you have to do is open the door.

"Welcome home, Captain Strovic, you have a lot to think about."

With that the "not a real frog" disappeared in a little puff of not-smoke.

FORGOTTEN KNIGHTS

Mattom Caradalf looked up at the crenellated walls of the castle keep. The imposing pink-granite ramparts seeming to descend slab-sided and sheer from the very heavens themselves. Like banners of war hung from the undersides of the angry clouds, these fortified walls were a massive statement of permanence and strength, forbidding and dark - and about as much use against heavy laser fire as a chocolate snod bat.

Mattom sighed and leaned with his arms folded against the hood of his space-boat. Two weeks since he had arrived, assigned with the job of trying to organize a defence, and he had come to the inevitable conclusion that there was no way that the company office contained within the castle could withstand a hi-tech take-over from the Sirburlaki-K Corp.

The budget allocated to planetary defence by his own company, Arcturus Ice, had only just about stretched to renting him a jump-boat to get him out to the lost planet of McLuhan.

It had been four hundred years since Arcturus Ice had acquired McLuhan. The swampy planet was part of the settlement of the first Scorpius war but, due to a foul-up at the regional office, the deeds had never been processed. Although an initial colony team had been sent, no back up had ever followed on. No building materials, no FTL transmitter, no communications, supplies or personnel.

Once they had figured out the situation, the original development team managed to send a radio signal of sufficient power to reach head-office, but without FTL the radio wave had taken four hundred years to reach the nearest receiving station.

Unfortunately for Arcturus Ice, Sirburlaki-K Corp had also picked up the transmission, and realized that an unprocessed deed of planetary possession could be theirs for the price of an assault squad and a team of salvage lawyers.

Mattom looked around from where his boat was parked in the castle's main courtyard.

"You'll just have to improvise with whatever you find when you get there." His manager, Kimry Bunnin, had said taking her usual sympathetic line.

*

The truth was that Mattom had had no idea what to expect at all. In four hundred years the colony might have failed altogether, or developed in any number of unpredictable ways. He had spent the trip out to McLuhan trying to figure out what a group of humans could get up to if left on their own for four centuries.

However, even in his wildest musing, what Mattom expected had at no point involved knights in armour and castles.

"Aha, there thou art," called out the heavily accented voice of Lord Silvas Boht, the current holder of what had become the hereditary position of Company Rep.

"When thou didst tell of the perfidious intentions of the dread Sirburlaki-K I did raise the militia, and every thane of the Divine Company of Arcturus Ice now dons their best armour and musters to our banner."

"Great," growled Mattom. "Your tin-clad farmer boys against the best hired-lasers money can buy."

"The words from thy mouth are unclear to me, yet their tone is not. Thou doubtest our strength and our will." Lord Silvas was a large man. The huge black cuirass that covered his chest gave him the appearance of someone wearing a cast-iron stove.

Mattom looked up at the grizzled older man.

"I'm sorry, Lord Silvas. It was not my meaning to say anything bad about you or your knights, but they are no match for the forces that come this way."

Lord Silvas laughed.

"Then we shall fight against the odds, there can be no greater kudos." A sharp glimmer lit his eyes. "We shall see soon enough, scouts report a small group of strangely clad men, six in a company, that come hither to our fastness. They bring with them a large device, no doubt a siege engine. They may be the best warriors that Sirburlaki-K can put into the field but we shall sally forth and take them by surprise, scattering them to the star winds."

"Yeah yeah, whatever," said Mattom through a sigh.

He spent the next few hours with Lord Silvas, organizing the farmers as they drifted in from the fields, assembling them in the courtyard of the castle. They all wore the same black armour. It looked like cast iron, no protection at all against the high-tech lasers of the opposing company. Mattom did what he could with them, telling them how to find and keep to cover.

Finally, as the lookout on the battlements raised a cry, Lord Silvas approached Mattom, leading two horses by the reins.

"You have travelled far to be with us on this glorious day, it would not be fair for me to neglect our honoured guest from the Divine Company. Ride with us and share the glory as we strew the enemies of Arcturus Ice before us."

"Ah...." said Mattom. "Now...I'd really love to Lord Silvas, but I usually stay at the back in these kind of things...It's in my contract you see." Mattom was about to go on and explain, when Lord Silvas grabbed his right hand and thrust the reins of one of the horses into his surprised grasp.

"I won't tell if you don't," he said, but there was a look in his eye that explained the situation to Mattom much more clearly than words could manage. "And here is your armour." The Lord produced a leather belt with a small red box attached; a dimple switch labelled "on/off" was all the markings it had. Mattom looked in deep puzzlement at what he was holding, and as he did so, Lord Silvas slipped the leather shoulder ties of his cuirass and let the metal armour drop to the ground. Mattom saw that all the other knights had done the same.

"What are you doing?" A faint note of desperation crept into his voice.

"Have you not said that this armour will not prevail against the guns of Sirburlaki-K?"

Mattom nodded, dumbstruck.

"Then what profit in wearing it? No, we shall don our best, and ride out in our dress armour. If we must lose, we will look good doing it. Now come, fasten thy belt, 'tis time to mount."

Mattom fastened the belt with trembling fingers and, under the watchful eye of Lord Silvas, he mounted the horse, then he and all the other knights lined up ready to charge out as the drawbridge was dropped.

A bugle sounded. The farmers began to ride across the clattering wood of the drawbridge. Lord Silvas raised his arm and shouted "Armour on." The farmers pressed the switch on their belts, and Mattom followed suit. Nothing seemed to happen, but as Mattom looked about him, the scruffy farmers had disappeared. In their place now rode fifty perfect knights that seemed to have ridden straight from some ancient myth. The belts they all wore projected a hologram of flawless silver armour.

Before him across the scrub, Mattom caught his first sight of the Sirburlaki-K assault squad. Six laser armed soldiers flanked to guard a heavy laser canon. The first shot was fired, and Mattom looked around expecting to see a knight fall, but none did.

"Must have missed," he had time to think. Then another shot was fired and another and another; a volley of laser fire opened up from the seasoned troops of the Sirburlaki-K company. Still no knight fell. At the same moment both Mattom and the Sirburlaki-K soldiers realized the truth. The hologram projectors wrapping the knights in their armour were acting as perfect mirrors. The lasers were bouncing off without harm. They might as well have been armed with flashlights. The soldiers saw the charging horses coming towards them and, taking almost a whole second to decide, as one they dropped their weapons and ran as fast as they could.

Two hours later, Mattom was back in the cabin of his jump boat, tracking the soldiers as they left orbit. Things were suddenly looking good for Mattom. The planet still belonged to Arcturus Ice, and they had managed to salvage a top of the line Sirburlaki-K heavy laser cannon. "He might even get a little bonus for this," he thought.

Lord Silvas poked his head around the door of Mattom's jump boat.

"Just before you go, a quick question. About back-pay actually. Four hundred years worth of back pay to be precise."

"Ah…" said Mattom.

TEMPUS FUGIT

The tug was the usual sort of thing that you'd expect from the Rimworlds Corporation, squat, short, and with the kind of endearing ugliness that functionality can impart to unadorned industrial designs. She had been assembled around the central component of the brutally powerful UltimaThrust Model 40 lifting engine, and there was very little excess room in her overstuffed skin for anything else, including crew quarters.

Three claustrophobic and dull weeks since the *Kwantah* had cast her moorings at Caderil Deep-Dock, and finally she had arrived at the unscheduled drop-off point for her two unwelcome passengers.

The tug settled ungracefully into an approach vector for RtanZ132, a minimum priority outworld owned by the ENL Corporation. From space, great storms could be seen stirring up the deep and dark oceans of this wild looking backwater planet. Ramparts of cloud massed below the incoming ship, marking the fortress wall of a violent hurricane.

Cardhean Marf sat in one of the two tiny view port blisters, enduring the cramped conditions of the ship, and the incessant conversation of his travelling companion, Bidfol Varp.

"We won't be coming down through that, will we?" Bidfol said again for the third time, staring out of the view-port at the fast approaching world. Whenever the weight of his companion's silence became too much, Bidfol would allow some part of his mental process to leak out as if there had been a conversation. Cardhean screwed up his features as the white star of the RtanZ132 system swung across the view dome, indicating a sudden change in the attitude of the ship.

"No," he said at last. "The xeno-site is on the other side of that large ocean, we should miss the low pressure area."

The *Kwantah* was making her final manoeuvres before the captain brought her slicing down through the atmosphere. The two Paloxenologists had only managed to get their place aboard the ship at the last moment, and had been lucky to arrange that. The crew of the Kwantah had been contracted to help with the erecting of a permanent orbital-elevator site on Baxtil, and pressure from the Imperial Science Service had persuaded the Rimworlds corporation to delay her departure until Cardhean and his assistant could arrive from the Alop dig site on Parras.

The older of the pair considered his younger companion. Bidfol had finally fallen silent as the increasingly detailed view over the rapidly approaching world took his breath away. Cardhean knew that Bidfol had his faults, talking too much being chief amongst them, but he also knew that the youngster had a good soul, not to mention a sharp grasp of the subject.

"Cardhean!" He pointed towards the planet's surface. "Are those rectilinear structures?" Cardhean looked where Bidfol was indicating.

"Roads from the Turkam Empire period," he said, "about seven thousand years old. This planet has colonisation periods for all the major cultures of the last ten thousand years. It was a world of strategic importance for a very long time." He turned to his companion. "It makes our own thousand year career as space farers seem rather insignificant, does it not?"

The tug rattled and shook and grumbled her way through the atmosphere, until with a last sputter of her vast engine, she settled in mind numbing silence onto the decking of a landing pad.

The captain came and personally escorted them to the docking port. She was obviously relieved to get them off her ship, and showed barely concealed pleasure in handing over responsibility for her charges to the planet's Harbour Master.

The view of the surface of the world that greeted them as they left the ship was no less dramatic than it had been from orbit. The up-site was on the coast of one of the main landmasses of the northern hemisphere. Cardhean and Bidfol had arrived in the middle of the local winter. The sea that pounded against the black rocks of the iron coastline was organic and grey. She moved like a great beast, and the small yellow sun hid behind the clouds, flaming the horizon with her dying rays.

"Darkness lasts about fifteen hours at this time of the year," said the Harbour Master, "which should give you a reasonable crack of daylight to get over to the drill site tomorrow."

The facilities of the up-site were basic, but compared to the privations of the last three weeks, the frontier station felt like an exotic palace of strange pleasures, chief amongst them being washing and solid food. Cardhean succumbed to the effects of a good meal and slept the uninterrupted sleep of the just.

*

The conveyance that arrived for them early the following morning was as ugly and functional as the tug had been. There was, however, a more comfortable cabin. They were being taken out to the drill site on the back of one of the giant ore transporters. Great wheels, as tall as the spindly trees of the sodden coastal morass, rolled slowly over the vast moors and bogs of these waterlogged northern lands. The sky was unked and low, clouds roiling with the anger of a world without servants.

To Cardhean, the view from the balcony of the passenger compartment was cold and bleak. The metal grey sky touched his eyes and chilled his soul. Bidfol shivered, but stayed outside, gripping the rail and absorbing the world. He was seemingly immune to the desolation that stretched from horizon to horizon.

Occasionally the skeletal remains of a structure would rise bleached and incomplete from the greeny yellow of the endless cold grassland. Bidfol would point, and say something like "Tukkai'yyid?" and Cardhean would either confirm the identification, or point out the diagnostic markers that would mean that it was something other.

"Although the fascia markings resemble first dynasty Tukkai'yyid decorative architraves, if you notice that the uprights show eight reinforcing rods, of a twisted pattern, then the only conclusion is that it has to be from the IrTakeen period that directly followed on from the collapse of the Takkai'yyia homeworld, and was actually up to a thousand years later."

They had been travelling like this for nearly half a day when Bidfol suddenly pointed and yelled out to Cardhean:

"Gribbler!"

"Where?" answered Cardhean. Bidfol pointed over the balcony and Cardhean saw them. The creatures were grey and twice as big as the Gribblers at home, but they were, without a shred of a doubt, Gribblers.

"Even out here on the rim," said Cardhean.

The Gribbler was found on every habitable world so far discovered. That, by itself, would have been remarkable enough, but creatures of the Gribbler genus were also found on his own home-world, and also those of every other sentient species that made up the Communion of Stars.

Throughout the history of every known world, Gribblers had been kept as pets, hunted for food, farmed and culled, but they were everywhere. Nobody knew on which world they had evolved, or how it was that they had come to be spread all across the galaxy, from heart-stars to spirals' end. It was merely one of those things that had to be accepted, as the answer lay beyond the horizon of retrievable knowledge.

"What the hell *are* those things?" Cardhean wondered. The question was only half aloud and addressed to himself, but Bidfol was never one to miss an opportunity to express his own opinion.

"A test of faith," he said flatly. The words were such a bold statement that Cardhean took a moment or two to absorb the importance.

"Explain." he said. This was something in Bidfol's character of which he had had no previous inkling.

"Every Quilpo knows that Gadrean is the home of life, and the special world of creation. Every Irtakee knows that the Tukkai'yyia created their species on Palava, and that Palava is the chosen world. Every species knows that they have a special

relationship with the universal creator." Cardhean was fascinated, Bidfol clearly had
thought of this over many years. The words when he spoke them had the familiarity
of frequent rehearsal.

"Eventually all of the 'special' species make their way into space and they find
that there are thousands of habitable worlds scattered across the skies and that there
is life on all of them; their uniqueness suddenly wiped away by the reality of the
crowds of life. Some species are similar, some share the basic building blocks, and
some can barely recognise each other as life forms. Yet on all these worlds, even the
home-worlds, there are Gribblers." He looked as if he was coming to the point of
his argument.

"The Gribblers are messengers from God. He created life everywhere, and every
life-form is part of God's design for the universe, great and small, concrete and ethe-
real, and they're all so different; the Gribblers are a sign that it is all the work of the
same divine hand. They are like his signature on the grand canvass. 'I made this'".

Cardhean leaned back shocked, and after a while he relaxed.

"I've heard worse," he said, "but I'd keep that particular theory to yourself when
we get back to the Institute. The scientific method has some especially rabid follow-
ers on the finance committee. You may find funding a little harder to come by if they
think you have anything even remotely spiritual in your make-up."

Bidfol looked shocked. "I'm not a follower. I didn't sound like one, did I?"

"We are nervous of people that talk about god," said Cardhean sternly, "it has
lead to too much grief between those very species that you claim are all part of the
same creation. With views like that, you're just as likely to be strung up by believers as
scientists, so keep 'em to yourself."

"Yes Master Cardhean, I will take your advice."

Cardhean nodded seriously. He was always rather gratified at the fact that Bidfol
never knew when he was winding him up.

They rolled on across the moors until Cardhean spotted the white masts of the
ENL station in the distance. As they drew closer, they could see the loading bay for
the ore transporter and the drill site. This was the reason that they had travelled the
width of a spiral arm in the back of a tug.

The weak sun was low on the horizon as they pulled into the outpost. The station commander that met them was obsequious and noticeably nervous. He offered
to take them to their rooms, but Cardhean none too gracefully insisted that they be
taken directly to the cavern.

The descent was via a cable lift, and the shaft was deep.

"You're sure of the dating?" Cardhean asked the Commander.

"There can be no room for doubt, Master Professor," he said. "The stratigrafy is
unbroken in this area. We are the first culture on this world to drill in this site, there is
no contamination, and the find is way below anything even the Consus culture could
have created."

The drop shaft was small and square and descended deeply into the planet, until eventually the little car carrying the three entered a vast cavern that had been carved out by high power GABIL beams.

"How much damage to the site did the initial contact cause?" asked Bidfol when he saw the GABIL projectors.

"We turned off the gravity amplifiers as soon as we realised what we had found, but we were using heavy-G cutters, set to wide dispersal." He paused nervously, then obviously decided that truth would probably be less harmful to his career. "Compression damage is inevitable I'm afraid."

"Nobody could have expected such a discovery at such a depth," said Bidfol sympathetically. "Our report will be clear on that point." The base commander relaxed a little as the lift car came to a halt at the ground level.

"Welcome to forty-three million years ago," he said, ushering the two scientists into the vast and brightly lit cavern. The illumination came from floating spotlight platforms that drifted gently to-and-fro in the dusty air.

The anticipation that bit into Cardhean was almost unbearable. His emotions were powerful and mixed. His excitement at the magnitude of such a find was tempered only by an awe that was indistinguishable from terror - or, he tried to find exactly the right word to fit, and realised that what he felt was dread.

The base commander led them across the perfectly flat floor of the cavern. They threaded their way between the stacks and piles of commercial supplies that were needed for such a deep mine operation.

Near the edge, where wall met floor, Cardhean spotted the beginnings of a rough area, unfinished. This was the point at which the GABIL beams were turned off. This was it. His breath became a little shorter. He had heard, he had read the descriptions, but until he saw it for himself he could not really believe it.

"There," said the commander. "That's where it started." Cardhean looked, and for a few disappointing and baffling seconds he was unable to make anything out. Then he saw it, a dark stain across the surface of the rock. A stain that travelled in a straight line, and parallel to it, another, and between them at regular intervals, stains that indicated the presence of some long decomposed organic material running at right angles between the two straight lines.

"This was where it started, and we followed it along, for a way, thinking it was some mineralogical feature." The commander picked up some lamps from a nearby crate, passing them to Cardhean and Bidfol. A tunnel had been carved around the straight-line feature, disappearing into the darkness of the deep past. Cardhean led the way. As they followed the lines into the passageway, the commander spoke.

"We followed the lines back, thinking that it might be a curiosity of nature, until we got to this point."

Cardhean froze. Another set of lines split from the first set and disappeared into the tunnel wall.

"When we found this," said the base commander, "we knew that we had to inform someone. I know it sounds crazy, but it looked to us like we'd found a fossilised railroad."

"Hmmm," said Cardhean. "Apart from the fact that the metallic deposits are not strictly speaking fossils, I'd be hard put to disagree with you."

*

The three of them stayed by the feature for a considerable time, but eventually Cardhean needed the communications system.

The base commander took them back to the surface and gave Cardhean and Bidfol the freedom of the installation. Cardhean sent a message to the Imperial Science Service, and waited impatiently for the answer. Three agonizing days and nights he had to wait until, on the dawn of the fourth day, the answer he had hoped for arrived.

The Imperial Heritage Fund had put a compulsory purchase order on the planet, and bought it from the ENL Corporation. It was now theirs. His entire staff were transferred, and several shiploads of equipment arrived over the following months. The base commander was loath to leave the world without knowing more, so Cardhean seconded him to his staff.

His team, under the careful scrutiny of Bidfol, widened the excavation, and the finds and the techniques that emerged from the site enthralled the galaxy.

They started by following the tracks back. The GABIL excavation of the cavern had eliminated the line of the track in the other direction, ruling out any progress down that route. The work to follow the rails took painstaking weeks. The skills to excavate a fossilised culture did not exist. Cardhean, Bidfol and the team were having to invent and improvise. They borrowed techniques more familiar to planetary engineers than xenologists.

Eventually the railroad led to a building that was obviously a temple, and that temple lead to other temples, and finally the outline of a town began to emerge from the petrified layers of time.

Cardhean made a crucial deduction. He concluded that there was evidence for different development strata, adding up to a history of fifty or sixty thousand years for this culture. The fragmentary stone implements that turned up in the increasingly massive excavation were dated to a much earlier period.

Eventually, as street after street emerged from their eons of concealment, it became clear that what they had exposed was nothing less that a fossilised city; a city that had lived and flourished for a period of perhaps three or four thousand years, roughly forty-three million years before.

The findings of the excavation were regularly making the news, and representatives of cultures from every arm of the galaxy were requesting access to the site. Cardhean's connections on the directorate of the Imperial Science Service meant that he was able to fend off unwanted interference, however, there were now a couple of naval vessels in orbit over the site, just in case.

The question that gripped every mind in the Communion of Stars was what had happened to these ancient ones. Fossilised life-forms were a regular part of the evolution of life-bearing rocky planets, but nowhere had anyone discovered any evidence of civilisation further back than a mere ten or twenty millennia.

It was the most frustrating experience of Cardhean's life. What was it that could have happened to them? Exciting as it was, there was nothing other than scraps of straight lines on which to build the story. Archaeology on his own world had been a frustrating experience, like a jigsaw with most of the pieces missing and no picture to act as a guide. Yet difficult as that had been, this was a quantum level beyond that. There were no objects to retrieve. This was more like finding a hint of the existence of some of the lines between the jigsaw pieces.

Then they found the spaceport. Cardhean would have missed it, but the base commander recognised the shape of an interspatial drogue projector as he watched one of the imaging screens. He had to trace the line several times before Cardhean saw anything except a lump of mud.

This culture had been space farers and city dwellers. Cardhean had been used to the past being able to talk to him. He could see the Tukkai'yyia, he could read about their achievements, he knew their gods, but this gulf of millions of years was unencompassable.

The second summer arrived, glorious and temperate. Cardhean had taken a tent into a local range of hills, with the idea of doing some fishing. Two days he had been hiking through the rugged landscape, appreciating the rivers and lakes of the high purple moor land.

He would not have voluntarily left the dig, but Bidfol persuaded him that his work was suffering, and that a short break would clarify his thoughts. Yet every waking minute his mind was turned to the world of the city. He looked around him, trying to imagine its vast sweep spread out across these wild lands, visualising the scene as it must have been forty-three-million years earlier.

He pitched his tent by the shore of a deep and still lake in a steep-sided valley. Tall pine trees grew in sociable clumps, and the warmth of the sunlight restored him somewhat.

A group of Gribblers were at first rather put out by his arrival, but after a couple of days convinced themselves that Cardhean was no threat. They quickly became confident enough to take back their favourite spot on the lakeshore.

These were much smaller than those he had seen on the first day, and as he watched them, he admired the skill with which they retrieved the large fresh-water tubeworms from the lake's edge. One of the Gribblers became sociable to the point that Cardhean and the small animal would have breakfast together. Cardhean relaxed and enjoying the view, the Gribbler sitting confidently on the edge of the table, squelching his way through a tubeworm that was almost as big as he was.

Bidfol contacted him on the fifth day.

"We have an organic fossil," he said without embellishment. Cardhean felt as if he had been electrocuted.

"How complete? How much have you got?"

"Pretty much a whole quarter of a skeleton. Half a jaw, most of a skull, several ribs, almost all of the spine, and an arm."

"I'll be there!" blurted Cardhean uncontrollably. "Send a transport for me, I need to be there now, Bidfol."

"It's already on its way, it'll be there by nightfall."

"Nightfall!"

"Best we can do, master," said Bidfol, and the regret in his voice convinced Cardhean that it was genuine.

"Send me the scans then, at least give me something to look at while I'm waiting."

"You should already have them." Cardhean cut Bidfol off without any formalities and went straight to the viewer.

The Gribbler watched all of this activity with a certain sceptical amusement. one leg stretched elegantly over the edge of the table.

Cardhean was trembling as he activated his portable; he was about to get his first look at the species that might be the creators of the city.

The images had been highlighted with false colour enabling him to immediately make out the shape of the body. Bilateral symmetry was the first obvious feature. As he took it in, he needed to know whether this was a member of the builder species or merely an associated animal. At the end of the arm was a slightly darkened band that passed over the wrist. Cardhean examined the scan for a moment, trying to think what might have caused such a thing, and then he realised that it was metallic oxidation staining. The only possible explanation was jewellery.

There was something unsettlingly familiar about the skeleton, but Cardhean was unable to identify it immediately. He looked up briefly, and his glance took in his breakfast companion and the confident way that the little animal held his meal. The single opposable digit, the pollex, was one of the fourteen diagnostic markers that unified all the species of Gribblers across the galaxy.

Cardhean increased the magnification of the hand. Four segmented digits, and underneath, only visible once he had begun to look for it, a fifth in opposition to the others.

Cardhean had a click moment, where difficult becomes easy, and obscure becomes clear.

"No!" he shouted. The word was denial and astonishment in one syllable.

The Gribbler looked at him and uttered the single sound that comprised its complete vocabulary.

"Mook?"

Cardhean was stunned, awash with emotions that could not even be labelled. He sat back, trying to take in the weight of his thoughts.

He stared at the image. He had found a missing piece of the jigsaw, and suddenly he understood the whole, but the picture that he had struggled so long to put together, struggled so hard to encompass, was more desolate than his soul could bear.

A chill wrapped around him. The sunlight no longer had the power to warm him. The strength left him as if he had been assaulted. He looked from the scan to the Gribbler and back to the scan. Fourteen diagnostic markers, and as he looked closer he was able to check off the half dozen or so that were not related to soft-tissue structures. The skeleton with the bracelet was without doubt a Gribbler. Substantially different in appearance to the friendly little creature that shared his breakfast table, but without doubt a Gribbler.

The full weight of what the fossilised skeleton meant hit him at that moment, and Cardhean felt as if his entire species had been informed that it had a terminal disease.

"It was you," he said, addressing the Gribbler. "Forty-three million years ago, your ancestors set off from this world, as intelligent as any species that the galaxy has ever seen, maybe more so. You reached the stars, you settled on every world we have reached so far, and who knows how many thousands of others. Your species spread throughout the galaxy. You built spaceports and railroads, you sailed the interstellar seas, successful beyond our imagining. And now I know, I know what happened to the ancients."

He stood and distractedly took a few wandering steps away from his campsite.

"It's all for nothing!" he blurted, the weight of the future pressing down on him. "All you did, all we will do, it's all for nothing. You can't stop evolving; in the end, there are Gribblers everywhere, intelligence is no longer a survival factor. You evolved beyond the need for brains." Cardhean turned his gaze to the heavens.

"I thought that the end of evolution would be to become creatures of intellect and energy, transcendent, indistinguishable from the angels." He turned back and regarded the Gribbler, the repository of the complete genetic history of the human race.

The little animal was the descendant of Shakespeare and Lao Tzu, Einstein and Sargon of Akkad, and millions of others, from the hundreds of thousands of years of the human dominated galaxy. The Gribbler, the latest of the sons of Adam, the inheritor of the Earth, stared back at the scholar.

"Mook?" he said, and took another bite of his tubeworm.

SELF PORTRAIT WITH BANDAGED EAR

The Crystal Beasts of Planet Fairlight were the happiest creatures anywhere in charted space. Great herds of the bovinoid ruminants wandered the plains of their native world in contented groups called "Lu-kneis". It could take a Lu-knei two of the over-long days of Fairlight to pass a single point as they wandered in their constant search for fresh spongy forage.

The first human travellers were charmed by the playful nature of these flat footed and ungraceful looking cowoids, and after much study they realised that the Crystal Beasts actually engaged in a sort of dancing, and that the incessant noise that issued from them was in fact communication. Perhaps not as the people of Earth usually thought of it, but it seemed to do for the Crystal Beast's purposes.

The best telepathic linguists of the human realm were called in to see if the speech contained anything meaningful, or of import, but they were disappointed to discover that the substance of the language was restricted to "Oooh, look at the trees. Spongy Grass! I'm sooo happy it makes me want to sing."

Unfortunately, a promising junior linguist called Attila Lipschitzowichowskyanitch allowed himself to spend too much time in proximity to the Crystal Beasts' mind and lost his sanity after prolonged exposure to the unending cheerfulness. It was shortly after that that trouble really started.

At any given point there will be a human that looks at another species and has the thought, "I wonder what that tastes like." The innate happiness of the Crystal Beasts was a guarantee of tender and juicy meat, he reasoned, provided they could be slaughtered without upsetting them too much. Attila the linguist, a malcontent dropout from the University of Topanga, went native, living alone in the hills. The search for the perfect Crystal Beast became an obsession. He honed his skills with spear and knife, until for the first time in his life he was prepared and ready to go out on the hunt.

Working his way down from the hill where he had made his encampment, he

found one of the great Lu-knies on its annual migration across the plains. He could
smell the rank fishy aroma of the herd from half a kilometre away, and as he reached
the place where he had built his hide, the sound of the Crystal Beasts' tuneless singing
was almost deafening. Their thoughts in his head "I'm so happy, hap hap happy happy
hap hap happy, I'm so happy, hap…" Now he *really* wanted to kill one.

A young beast strayed a little too far from the herd and a little too close to his
hide. He grabbed his spear, and leapt out at it. His sudden appearance made the young
Crystal Beast visibly jump, and there was a brief moment of eye contact. He pulled
back his arm and he let fly with the spear. He caught his prey in the soft flesh below
the ribs, and he felt a sudden burst of searing pain coming from the creature, and then
the sound of the song changed.

The Crystal Beast cried out in its terror and its agony, and the sound of its completely alien pain was the sweetest refrain any human ear would ever hear. To the
Crystal Beasts of the Lu-knie, the cry was a warning and a scream; to the linguist it
was the song of the deep diving whale and the ascending lark, the sound of a summer breeze through sacred groves of cedar, the words "I love you" whispered in the
dark.

He leaned on the haft of the spear, pushing it further into the wound, and the
song became sweeter yet. Eventually the beast gave up its life to his shaft, and the
linguist sat on the spongy grass of the plain and wept. Not for the life he had taken
but for the end of the song his regret.

After some time he recovered himself, hauling the carcass onto the travois he had
prepared, and he dragged the meat up to his camp on the hillside. He butchered the
animal as best he could and roasted a great hunk of it over an open fire.

He had saved a bottle of good French red wine for the occasion, and with anticipation more intense than he had ever known, he sliced off a small piece of the meat
and put it in his mouth.

The consistency was perfect. Just as he had suspected the meat was tender and
moist. The relaxed life of the beast produced juicy muscle and not sinewy, stringy,
scraggy meat. The texture was heaven, but the flavour… the flavour…

His tongue felt as if it had been assaulted by the vilest collection of chemicals a
human palette had ever encountered. It was quite simply the most disgusting experience he had ever had. He could not believe the nauseating sensation of filth that
raged across his taste buds.

A sane mind might have given up at that point, a starving person might have
reached for the chilli sauce, but he was neither. He wanted to punish these creatures
for his lost sanity, for his inability to go back to his life as it had been, for the loss of
his future. He sat, forcing himself to take mouthful after mouthful of the revolting
flesh, washing it down with the wine, until as the pale blue sun rose over the plains he
finally had an idea that would turn him into one of the richest men in the galaxy.

With his remaining cash reserves he arranged for the importation of a pedigree
Hereford bull, and once more out on the plains he built a small enclosure. It was not

difficult to capture one of the Crystal Beasts; he simply sneaked up behind one when it wasn't looking.

He surrounded the enclosure with audio recording equipment. He had considered video but came to the conclusion that what he was planning would probably be better if the people listening did not know how the music was made.

He restrained his newly captured Crystal Beast so that she could not escape, and with a pheromone spray he turned her into an appealing mate for the bull.

The pain and the distress of the union immediately went to number one in the charts of fourteen planets. But that was not the end. With genetic manipulation the linguist had ensured that the forced congress would bear fruit. The chimera of the two species formed in the womb of the Crystal Beast, as heavy as its father, but the linguist had altered it so that the horns from its Earthly sire began to form even as its mother carried it. He made sure that his captive was given regular doses of pain enhancing chemicals, and the recording devices were left on twenty-seven hours per day.

Album after album of the most relaxing ambient style music issued from the Crystal Beast's unending agony. People on Earth would lay back and chill, visualising the peace and profundity of the ocean depths, or feel the stretched wings of eagles against a golden sky.

Eventually the unnatural offspring was ready. The Crystal beast could no longer contain the vile abomination within her body, and her contractions started. Her frame was never meant to contain the mass of her transgenic progeny, and the linguist was prepared to do nothing for her other than making sure that the pain enhancers were boosted to the max.

She was a wild creature, used to running on the unending plains, the small enclosure was an unnatural hell for her. Restricted and tethered, there was no escape from the attack that came from inside her own body. The head of the chimera began to force its way into the world, the horns gouging a path through the soft flesh of the birth canal. As body fluids spurted and bits of her soft tissues ripped and tore, her song became a crescendo of incredible sadness. No sane human could have been unmoved by the pathos of the sound. The linguist stared deep into its eyes and smiled.

The Crystal Beast convulsed suddenly. All of the muscles of her stomach went into deep spasm as the unfortunate creature tried to expel the calf, her legs kicking wildly, as if trying to run away.

The contraction took her whole body, and then abruptly, with a great, wet, ripping noise, her entire and vastly distended abdomen gave way, splitting open like a bursting pod. The implanted alien from Earth fell from the mortal wound, glistening, onto the spongy grass of Fairlight.

The linguist stared into her face as she died. Her last thought crossed his mind "Why?"

He reached down and tenderly closed her eyes.

"Why should I tell you?" he thought to her. "You either get it, or you don't."

He looked at the new arrival.

"Hello," he said, "I wonder what *you* taste like."

IGNORANTIA JURIS

There was always going to be a remote possibility of a time traveller turning up from the moment when the LHC went live, but judging by the looks on their faces I got the feeling that they weren't really expecting one.

Scientists are like that. They'll tell you they think something is possible, like time-travel or life on Mars, just to get you excited about funding them, but they don't really believe it themselves because they don't believe in magic. However, much as they'd have liked to, they were never able to find the bit in the details of the universe that would render spooky old time-travel impossible.

I arrived in a puff of something that looked like smoke and felt like semolina, standing with my briefcase held before me like a shield. For me, I neither need to believe nor disbelieve, I'm a lawyer, and on this trip I was a paying passenger of the Temporal Railroad Company of 2177.

If I had landed on target, I should be standing on the minus side of the Compact Muon Solenoid, under the main shaft. I looked around, still feeling queasy. The green paint of the aluminium inspection platform seemed impossibly bright and the smell of concrete and ozone was exactly like the mock up in the time station. I blinked a couple of times, and the relief forced the tension to let go of my shoulders. I had made it.

The LHC was the first machine to create subatomic temporal distortions, no good for time travel in themselves, but they formed the zero-datum point from which a time machine existed, and so the later technologies based on low-dimensional temporal geometry were able, theoretically, to exploit this as the end of a railway line. I say theoretically because in 2050, my year of travel, nobody had ever gone back that far. When I told the company my intended destination, they at first flatly refused.

"The LHC," they explained, "isn't so much the last station on the line, as the buffers at the end of it." It was all Geek to me, and they could throw as much of it at me as they liked. I had a place and a time and a very special client, and they were going to send me there, and my company was not one to be denied lightly.

My watch had already been set to local time, I had a little bit of running to do, then three minutes of hiding, before I could walk out on the back of a tour group. My briefcase contained everything I needed to blend into the background. I was amazed at the calm faces of the staff I saw as I moved around the place. They had built this completely amazing machine, the LHC, designed to throw energies around on a scale previously never envisaged, and they had no expectation of anything amazing happening, like for example a lawyer from a future falling out of a wormhole.

I had planned my exfiltration based on camera timings and security logs from the online archive. I was particularly keen not to get caught. I hadn't come back forty years to spend the next forty rendered to an existence-denied prison somewhere extraordinary.

Aside from a few technological items that were meant to ease my escape from Switzerland, my briefcase was also full of period traveller's cheques and temporally valid ID, so relatively easily I left CERN behind and made my way to Amsterdam.

I knew where to find her because of the arrest records. I got there about an hour before she was due to be raided for drugs.

Her name was Barbi Bodega, and she was worth all the risks. She was lead singer of Franken Ken. I leaned on the bell until she emerged into the pale summer sunlight. She stood in the doorway, a cigarette drooping from her famous pout and a child held to her hip. She was just the way she was in the photos, her hair bleached and dyed so many times that the texture was like carpet, her skin corpse white, and she smelled of vomit and English gin.

"Consider yourself served," I said, giving her the papers. She squinted at the summons.

"I'm being sued?" Her voice, contralto and wrecked by alcohol, broke with the surprise. "What for? Who by?"

I reached out and tickled the baby's chin.

"Barbi Bodega 2050," I said.

"What?" She really didn't have a clue. Nothing like the woman I remembered.

"Barbi Bodega in 2050 is sixty-two years of age," I said. "She is a radically different person to you, and she has inherited the body that you created for her, and all the medical problems that entails. To be honest I can't see her surviving another summer like the last one. And she wants what you owe her, another twenty years of life. So she's suing you for reckless endangerment and is applying for sequestration of all the profits from your last two albums.

"You're having a laugh ain'tcha? Lawyer from the future, no such thing."

"Oh I admit, this will be the first time your legal system has come across one, but I have been the temporal specialist with Boylett Wisty and Grole for the last twenty years, and most of the legislation I need is already in place. The Temporal Bar Association calls it accidental case-law. Trust me on this, I'm going to win, and my Barbi Bodega is going to get what the people that care about her really want for her…more life."

"But you can't take all of my money. How am I going to live? I've got a kid now, how am I supposed to look after him?"

I turned and walked away.

"Don't worry about him," I said. "He grows up to be a lawyer."

TICK TOCK CURLEY WURLEY

Professor Michelle Tartuffe examined her reflection in the black glass of a fluorescent night-time bus ride. She insisted on taking the bus home, and the White House insisted that she did not. Seventy-three inches from her Chaco sandals to her wild hair, the Prof knew that she stood out in any crowd, and when she spoke she had an accent, Haitian, with a hint of the rhythms of France. However it was English that was her first language and she spoke it with elegance and precision. Her diction was clear, her vocabulary extensive and her enunciation always deliberate, and yet… and yet.

Whenever she talked to one of C M Kornbluth's *Marching Morons*, any one of the random, undereducated ferals that seemed to have invaded her intelligent world, the first barely articulated utterance that dribbled out as a slack-jawed reply to any attempt at communication was always the same.

Initiating contact with an easy to comprehend opening question, she would address the pierced moron in the Slip Knot shirt, saying something like, "Hi, do you know how long 'til the bus comes?"

Or…

To the bling bedecked moron on the table next to her in JavaStar, "Could you pass me the sugar please?"

And the reply from all genders and races of moron was always based around the theme of "Wha…?"

This now formed a very basic part of the Prof's diagnostic markers for determining intellectual status. If the first reply to a communication was a request to repeat the initial statement due to lack of understanding, she knew straight away that she was dealing with a moron.

*

Since the turn of the century, Professor Tartuffe had been getting paid a small Washington-fortune for thinking aloud. She had published a paper extrapolating from a basic concept of super-intelligence and how to deal with first contact with super-intelligent races.

Stephen Hawkin's assessment of the situation was that given our own experience with colonization, any first contact with more advanced aliens would be more likely to resemble the movie Independence Day, than Spielberg's ET. Prof Tartuffe agreed, which was why she sat on the bus chewing distractedly on the nail of her right thumb.

First contact, when it came, had been unmistakable. The aliens had not spoken only to a few bespectacled computer geeks hanging out in the Central American jungles parcelling out data-packets to like-minded geeks everywhere. No, first contact had stopped the world and given it a good rocking. Every radio, every television, every terminal, every laptop and mobile phone had received the transmission. Every screen that could show words did, and everything that could make a sound spoke.

TICK-TOCK Curley-Wurley.
TICK-TOCK Curley-Wurley.

And that was it. That was the whole of the message. The transmission was non-directional, appearing to arrive from every-which-way simultaneously, and the best brains on the Earth, as well as television presenters, were stumped as to what the words actually meant. It was clear that the message was for humanity as a whole, not just the few elite governmental high-ups, but it was equally clear that humanity as a whole had no idea what was just said.

Once he had been convinced that the transmission was not some Earth-based hoax, the President's first instinct was to find a way of broadcasting a reply. Prof Tartuffe was the head of the appropriate think-tank, so suddenly she found herself on the great carpet of the oval office, explaining to the Secretary of State, who in turn re-explained to the President, that a technology gap of more than about two hundred years would render communication difficult, - and if these aliens were super-intelligent, then impossible - unless such advanced creatures were prepared to take the time to talk to us the way we do to cats and dogs.

*

"Look at it this way, Mr. President," she said. "First contact with an equal is in essence no different to when you see someone you like at a party. You think that you would like to get to know them. You then have to formulate a small and pithy first contact statement that will both pique their interest and elicit an open ended response allowing further communication."

"So what you are saying, Professor, is that this alien message is actually nothing more than a cheesy pick-up line."

The Prof smiled. "Actually, Sir, although the message may be seen as having an analogous purpose, it's probably more complicated than that."

"Yes," said the president, looking at his fingers. "Almost everything seems to turn out that way."

"What do you think the message actually means?" the Secretary of State asked, eyes sharp and alert. "Is it a McLuhan-esque test of reasoning where the words actually have no meaning, the mere existence of the transmission being its own message?"

Prof Tartuffe shrugged.

"As yet I have no real idea. For example, what goes tick-tock?"

"A clock," said the President.

"A bomb," said the Secretary of State.

"And our DNA is wrapped around in a double spiral, Curley-Wurley fashion. It could be that the message is saying something along the lines of "Shame about your genetic time-bomb". Or it might be that the whole message is nothing more than someone bending over and clapping their hands together, like when you call a dog over."

"Why don't we just ask them what they meant?" said the President.

"No," said the Prof vehemently, a look of blind panic on her face. "Our future survival is staked on our reply. We must figure it out, whatever it takes."

*

She rode the bus home. The stars had tapped the Earth on the shoulder, and it was up to her to make sure that humanity's answer was not "Wha…?"

Her reflection in the window held her gaze. "Tick-Tock Curley Wurley," she said. *Tick-Tock Curley Wurley.*

THE CLOTH FROM WHICH SHE IS CUT

Hain

Thessaly Orbital Processing Platform, five kilometres from edge to edge and half a kilometre deep, industrially huge, yet in scale it seemed nothing more than a mote of dust drifting above the muddy immensity of planet Faker's Head. And microscopic against the bulk of the orbital platform, an even smaller speck fled the refinery at full blast; the privateer vessel *The Morrigan*.

An old converted Cocos-de-mer class coloniser under the command of Anne Goldeneyed, *The Morrigan* bled out a desperate rainbow of energy fields as her wake. Steam, clouds and fireworks from an old drive pushed too hard, her escape brushing an iridescent arrow across the heavens.

Two frigates as escort, the *Epona* and the *Hecate*, stayed tight at the vessel's prow. The fleeing ships left the shadow of the dark-side, and Anne's display showed the first edge of the sun erupting like a diamond volcano over the shoulder of the world behind her.

Anne Goldeneyed watched, eyes wide, cold and angry, from her command chair on the bridge of *The Morrigan*. The Faker's Head was a twenty-five solar-mass giant star with seven planets in the system, and Anne's Morrigan ignored them all.

She was beating for the companion star about a light-hour out from Faker's Head. This second sun, called The Cobra, was smaller even than Sol. The Cobra had exactly what Anne needed: polar jets.

With a couple of delicate finger waves through the control interface, she ordered her escorts to dock. Hangar doors slid open down the central spire of *The Morrigan* and the two frigates matched up and hooked on.

"Phase shield," Anne shouted across to Nancy Kurita.

"Aye, sir."

The phase shielding activated, adjusting the quantum modulation of *The Morrigan* so the old ship slid slightly sideways out of the universe.

The Morrigan eased her way into the ionic torrent of energy that blasted out from the surface of the small star. The Cobra was an anvil under the relentless magnetic hammer of the Faker's Head and the polar jets were a scream in the language of the stars.

Anne unwound from the command chair and, without a word to the bridge-crew, went to her cabin. She had not realised how clenched she had been. Her muscles protested as she climbed down the ladder to her quarters. Life had unexpectedly become very serious for the master of *The Morrigan*, and the stress was a weight on her shoulders that felt as if somebody had turned the gravity up.

She and her crew had, until this current debacle on Thessaly Station, made a profitable living between the less well defended cracks at the edges of the human sphere.

Born to a life of indenture on New Skye, Anne Goldeneyed endured thirteen standard years as property. A life filled with abuse and contempt taught her that to live meant to steal. So it was that three weeks before her warranty expired, and in the same way that the wolf steals the life of the rabbit, she slit the throat of the Gang-Master that owned her.

She had been running ever since, but Anne Goldeneyed lived her life without permission or dispensation.

She reached the base of the ladder and her cabin door sighed open. The room was small, tidy, and mostly brown.

Anne's problems were manifold. Fuel for her ships was scarce, the coffers were low, supplies were running out but most serious of all, the Faker's Head In-system Revenue Service had declared her ship, her holdings and all her possessions a taxable resource, on pain of death.

Anne Goldeneyed looked up and around. She needed to leave the Asclepiad system immediately, to get out of Dodge and lay low, particularly after the latest incident on Thessaly Station.

She sucked her teeth in loud disgust at herself. She had always stuck by the single tenet that you don't mess with the government, and now nowhere in system was safe for her because she broke her own golden rule.

She sat on the edge of her bunk, pinning her hands between her knees, her shoulders hunched up, her feet balanced on tip-toe so that they caught her twitch point. Anne stared at the window ahead of her, the muted golden glow of the Cobra still slightly visible through the opaqued transparent material. She realised that she was holding her breath and, with a sigh, she let her shoulders relax.

The alien object on her bedside table caught her eye and momentarily distracted her. She leant forward and picked it up again. As always, she felt the back of her hand prickle. The object was a simple silver wand. No external markings gave any kind of clue as to its purpose.

This little mystery had come into her possession the way that everything else in her life had: she had taken it from the weakening grasp of a dying man. A man who gave up his life to her blade rather than tell her what the damn thing was.

It had puzzled her for several years. What was so special about this little icy piece of metal that was worth hiring her to find, and dying to protect? Even the man who had employed her for the job had proved as silent as the grave he now occupied. However, his sacrifice had been a vain one. She finally knew. At last, she knew the secret that the silver rod contained.

The tingling she felt when she touched it was the interface of an alien technology. This sliver of alien metal had been crawling around inside her brain from the start, trying to tell her everything that she wanted to know, and one day, like learning a language by listening, she had woken up and the device had attuned itself to her thoughts.

The alien thing, brought alive by her touch, squirmed in her mind. Without appearing to project anything, the wand began showing her a recording of a sprawling and completely empty city. The moving images filled all the free space in her cabin. They showed tall, shimmering and obviously abandoned structures, elegant and slim. Spires that seemed to touch the yellow skies above them, shining with a metallic blackness that chilled her bones as she looked at them.

She had seen this city many times now, but the device knew what it was she was waiting for. Suddenly she was flying over the surface of this desert planet, skimming across the seemingly endless rolling dunes of an ocean of sand. After breasting one last rise, the ground plummeted away in a vertigo-inducing fall. The dunes replaced by the steep sides of an opencast mine, a gigantic scar on the surface of the world. A crimson wound against the yellow.

Anne recognised Cinnabar, the red gold of the new federation. The wand was showing her a treasure in the life-blood of space-farers. Every ship that plied the velvet depths between worlds had a core of Mercury, and what she was seeing was more wealth than all the fuel in the Stibnian Protectorate.

Anne looked at the untold kilometres wide cliffs of the red rock, and could not quite take it in. The depth of the excavation was phenomenal, the terraces stretched away as far as she could see. Nowhere in charted space had a rocky planet produced cinnabar in such obviously abundant quantity. The invitation to go and find this bounty was unambiguous, yet there was something in the chill, alien touch of the device that engendered in her a terror, a dread that went deeper than a mere fear of death.

She had so many doubts and questions. Who had made this map? Where had the invitation come from? Why was it sent? Was it real, and even if it was, how old was it?

Deactivating the device with a thought, she slipped it into the top pocket of her blouse and stood unseeing, staring out from her darkened window. The phase fields of her ship were at max, trying to keep an interspatial threshold between the living flesh of *The Morrigan*'s crew and the raw force of the surging solar-stream.

It was all moot anyway, she thought. Without any form of comparative stellar cartographical information, she had no way of knowing where this treasure planet was.

Anne brought her mind back to her current problems. *The Morrigan's* power plant could probably sustain sufficient output for a day maybe two, but she knew that her choices were severely limited and that the noose was likely already closing around her. She had to make a run for the bow-wave now and hope she could pick up a crumple on the other side. Anne needed to put some light-years between herself and her problems with the IRS.

The solar wind from the dwarf star glowed like liquid gold where it hit the shields. The focus returned to Anne's gaze, the thoughts cleared from her head, and the decision was made. She turned her back on the window and crossed her small cabin in three steps. The door scarcely had time to react to her sudden movement and barely swished open in time.

Her quarters lay directly below the main bridge of *The Morrigan* and were connected by an old fashioned ladder. She emerged behind her command chair and threw herself into its familiar leather with renewed energy.

"Mr Kurita," she shouted. "Follow the jet out as far as the heliopause."

"Aye, sir," said the PCD in the pilot's bucket. Anne opened a channel to her two escort vessels.

"We're moving out but stay docked, prepare all ECM and stealth systems."

The Morrigan started to shudder as the main in-system drive began ramping up the power.

Anne felt the ship, her ship, and she listened to its familiar noises as a conductor listens to an orchestra. She felt each bump and clank, as if she was part of the hull. Her senses were at full stretch, looking for anything unusual, the slightest sign of anything wrong. There was nothing.

As the engine came up to power, the shuddering died away and she was able to relax back into her seat a little.

"Active sensor!" came the shout. "IRS destroyer pinging us at three light-minutes."

"Directed or general?" Anne wanted to know, having to raise her voice to get over the thunder of the engine.

"Tight beamed. It was a confirmation pulse."

"They've got lock," shouted one of the Blain twins.

"Weapons systems online. Activate all ECMs. Launch decoys," she barked. *The Morrigan* may have been an old ship, built around even older technology, but she still had a trick or two up her sleeve. Anne leaned forward in her command chair and swirled her fingers through its interface. A tactical mini-map appeared before her.

"Give me a broad spectrum ping," she shouted.

"Aye, sir," came the reply. *The Morrigan* briefly lit herself up across multiple spectra as every active sensor aboard pinged. It was a calculated risk, but she needed to find out if the destroyer was alone or was herding her towards an ambush.

"New contacts, bearing zero-zero at five light-minutes."

Anne could see them, dead ahead, a cruiser and two frigates. A soft fricative crossed her lips.

"How long before the destroyer is in firing range?" she called out.

"It's gaining a light-second per second, optimal firing solution in two minutes," answered whichever of the Blain twins was working the threat-board. This was not the first time Anne had been in a situation like this, but it was the first time she had warranted the attentions of a cruiser, and she knew that where there was a cruiser there were...

"Fighters!"

"Tag them now!" she ordered. There was a real sense of urgency on the bridge. The fighters were only vulnerable to tagging as they launched from the bays. As soon as they could get their ECMs on line there was nothing aboard *The Morrigan* that could pick them up again. There were a few silent seconds of intense activity as the small crew tried to log and tag the fighters as they launched. Weapons lock would keep them visible, and would be hard to break.

"How many did we get?" she shouted.

"Seven," came the glum reply.

"How many they launch?"

"At least twice that. We're dead. Shall I signal our surrender, captain?"

"After Thessaly?" She sounded incredulous. "Go to one hundred and ten percent on the main drive and come to heading," she looked down at her display briefly, trying to find an escape course, "55, 230."

The ship rocked violently as the phase shielding absorbed the full force of a blast from one of the fighters.

The Morrigan burst from the golden torrent of the solar wind, making her best speed. Weapons fire flashed ineffectively behind her, she was still out of range of the destroyer and the ionic tempest issuing from the sun absorbed most of the energy from the fighter fire. The bridge crew were able to tag another two of the little ships as they fired, and a further two as they broke free of the jet.

"Gunnery crews, open fire!"

Around the base of *The Morrigan* every hard-light, plasma and blast weapon opened up on the chasing vessels, a heavy rain of incandescence, a fountain of multicoloured death. One of the tagged fighters, caught by surprise, evaporated into a fireball of molten slag. The rest of the attack ships, outraged by the loss of their comrade, began concentrating their weapons fire on the main drive systems. They formed up in twos and started their runs, classic zoom-and-boom tactics.

Anne watched the shield status display. Every incoming blast sapped the field integrity, and these fighters were fast - faster than *The Morrigan*.

"Deploy the Dim-probe any time you like, Mr Kurita," she said, the tension in her voice well masked, but not completely.

"I've been scanning but we're in flat space, not so much as a crease."

"As long we stay Newtonian, we don't have a chance," Anne countered. "Find us something."

"Destroyer just cleared the jet," said the Blain twin.

"Get us out of here now." Her voice had a shrill edge.

For the first time she could feel a little panic. She moved her finger through the map and brought up the image of the chasing destroyer. The ship was dark, but the onboard systems of *The Morrigan* put a red highlight around the image. Anne found the icon almost hypnotic, the swaying cobra before the mouse.

"Optimal firing solution in ten seconds," said the Blain twin quietly. Anne's thoughts were desperate, her mind was searching for an escape, and none was available. The end of the battle was inevitable, and would not involve prisoners.

In her mind the alien thing squirmed again and she felt the familiar cold tingle, but this time in the skin of her chest, where the device still rested in the pocket of her blouse. She could feel it in her head, looking around, and she realised that it did not want to die either.

"Power surge in the main reactor!" said the other Blain twin, but she could see that for herself. The indicators jumped on her console, recalibrating the scale to show the soaring output. A change went through the hull of *The Morrigan*. The "whiumsh whiumsh" of the hard-light turrets, and the "fhoum" of the plasma canon abruptly ceased, and yet more disturbing to Anne, the ever-present vibration of the engine stopped. The bridge fell completely silent, even the air-conditioning units spiralled down into uneasy quiet. She looked around and found herself meeting the equally baffled gazes of the Blain twins.

"We are no longer accelerating," came the unnecessary confirmation.

"Thank you, Mr Kurita," said Anne, her voice too distracted to be sharp. She turned to the threat board. "Is this part of the attack or have we just broken down?" The sweet smile on her face made the Blain twin swallow real hard.

"Spatial distortion forming ahead!" announced Mr Kurita. Anne's attention snapped back to the main viewer.

"I thought you said this was flat space," she queried.

"I did. It was."

Ahead of the ship a ragged ellipse could be seen forming, a patch of space darker than the surrounding darkness. Anne looked down at her interface, then she swirled her finger through all the telemetry settings. Nothing was showing anywhere except the visual range.

"What is it?" she asked, not really expecting anyone to answer. "Whatever it is, it's getting closer."

A froth of white was beginning to form around the edges of the dark stain on space, and a distinct surface was beginning to form.

"Can we ride it? I mean can you get the Dim-probe into it?" There was a slight note of hope in her voice.

"I'm beginning to get some resolution on the nav scanner," said Mr Kurita. "I know it sounds impossible, but it reads as an interplanetary crumple."

"But we're in system." Anne sounded baffled.

"Torpedo launch," announced the Blain twin on the threat board. "And another … and another." He paused to make a quick calculation. "Impact in twenty-five seconds."

Before them Anne watched as the spatial anomaly, the unexpected crumple, surged like the angry sea crashing against black rocks.

"Take us into it, Mr Kurita," she ordered.

"I have no power, and no controls."

"Fifteen seconds to first impact."

Anne was helpless. The crumple was tantalisingly close, escape visible but unattainable.

"Ten seconds."

The view screen showed the smoking trails of the torpedoes. Each of the massive missiles marked on her display with a small red icon superimposed.

"Five seconds."

The mouth of the crumple, completely formed and stable, suddenly surged forwards towards the ship.

"Four…"

Anne could see the segmented body panels of the torpedoes. She could see the crest of the Faker's Head on the warhead section.

"Three…"

"Two…"

The mouth of the crumple surged forward and snatched *The Morrigan* from normal space. The torpedoes passed harmlessly where she had been. To the chase ships, it appeared as if *The Morrigan* simply disappeared.

Tain

Anne sighed deeply, feeling the metal tang of stasis fill her lungs. Judging by the stiffness in her shoulders, she must have come out of Phase Stasis about twelve hours ago. She tried to swallow for the first time, and it was as if someone had sandpapered the inside of her throat. With effort, she opened her eyes and watched as the milky cover of the Hard-Sleep pod drained to transparency, revealing the normality of her cabin.

Her external window was clear again, and she could see diamonds on velvet beyond. Cold and cruel stars set against the endless violence of normal space. Anne realised *The Morrigan* had dropped out of the crumple.

With a slight hiss, the pod released a stimjet and suddenly Anne Goldeneyed had a clear head. The glass dagger that seemed to be skewering her sinuses reminded her how much she hated stasis. The cover cracked open and her Hard-Sleep pod began to rise to a standing position. Anne half leaned, half lurched forward, and as she did so Nancy Kurita expertly reached out a hand and supported her arm as she stood. Anne took a couple of unsteady steps into the centre of the cabin.

"Good morning, Cap'n," she said.

"Where are we, Mr Kurita?" asked Anne blinking, trying to find the focal length for her eyes.

Nancy Kurita was one of Anne's PCD crew. PCD stood for Personality Construct Device, a recorded personality of a real bioform human, copied, including all their skill sets, memories and experience, and placed into a floating multifunctional utility platform with onboard power supply, decent network connections and software guaranteed loyalty.

"We emerged from crumple about twelve hours ago. Initial astrometry puts us in Little Bear system, about forty light-years from Faker's Head."

"How long was I out?" Anne asked, adding the word "Thanks" as Nancy handed her a steaming mug of butterfly milk.

"Few days shy of two month."

There was a moment of silence as Anne digested the information.

"How far from Fakers Head again?"

"Forty light-years."

"In two months? Twenty light-years per month?" Anne's voice contained as much croaky incredulity as was possible after revivification from stasis. The distance was way beyond that which the old ship should have been capable.

"You don't know the half of it yet," said Mr Kurita. "We emerge in-system. A long, long way in-system, eleven light-minutes from star, and five light-minutes from planet Little Bear. Whatever trick it was that you pulled back there; it was sodding good one."

Anne took a sip from her mug, the hot liquid working its restorative magic on her head.

"And we weren't followed? I mean, nothing came through the crumple behind us?"

Nancy shrugged by way of an answer.

"Clear screens all the way back to Faker's Head," she said. "But that mean nothing of course. Crap old ship, crap old scanners."

"Hey," said Anne feigning offence. "Crap old ship she may be, but she's *my* crap old ship, and I won't have you talk about the old lady like that."

Anne lifted her mug in salute as Nancy left. "Thanks for this, by the way," she said. "I'll be up in a few minutes."

A quick change and a shower later, she was standing once again on the bridge of *The Morrigan*, leaning with her arms crossed over the back of her command chair, taking in the view over a totally new and unfamiliar planet.

Her initial reaction as her eyes tracked across the desolate splendour below was that it was nothing special. Another nameless rocky wasteworld, one of an uncountable infinity of its like that littered the galaxy. Just one more boulder in space with nothing to see except endless dull dunes, and range after range of meaningless mountains.

However, despite the unpromising appearance, she felt a sense of anticipation, almost excitement, building in the pit of her belly.

This was the Cinnabar World from her map. This was the world of the abandoned city. This was the world that offered riches beyond the imaginings of the even most pathological human minds. Anne felt the pull of that wealth like a fishing hook in the chest. It had to be it … it had to be.

The first of the Blain twins emerged from the crew deck, a towel draped around his neck, his short blond hair still spiky from the shower.

"Good morning, Captain," he said, stifling a sigh that could have been a yawn.

"Morning, Richard," she replied without lifting her eyes from the readouts of the planet below.

"I'm Philip," he said, nothing but weary resignation in his voice. She fixed him with a cold stare.

"Don't complain or I'll have it tattooed on your forehead, alright?" she warned.

He smiled by way of an answer but Anne could see the delicious hint of uncertainty in his eyes.

"And give me a full passive scan," she called. "If there's a satellite grid here I want to see it before it sees us, oké?"

"Aye, sir," he said, sliding in behind the sensor desk. It took him longer to adjust his seat than it did to scan the planet ahead of them.

"Colonist GPS system, three birds, low resolution, low cost. No military function. Orbital spread and altitude suggest that surface activity should be all centred around an area on one of the southern tectonic plates."

Anne watched as Philip used the eyes and ears of *The Morrigan* to extend his senses into the sky above Little Bear.

"I'm only picking up emission signatures from the birds," he said. "No transmission. There's power and some native RF but no info-stream, down, up or out."

Anne sucked her teeth and pursed her lips in most unfeminine manner. The satellites above Little Bear were dead.

"Oké, I want to know why those birds are cold, stay on that.. There must be an uplink site down there somewhere." Anne was thinking aloud.

"Mr Kurita, Do we have manoeuvring control?"

"Aye, sir, all ship's systems are back online."

"Philip, put up your best guess for the position of the colony."

A small pink blob began to pulse on the display of the planet. The other Blain twin emerged from the crew deck.

"Get on tactical," said Anne in her best managerial tone. "Emission control is the priority, make sure that no-one down there sees us coming, alright?"

Richard Blain nodded and got straight to work, casually walking through the main display of the planet to get to his position. Anne dipped a finger into her nav mini-map and dragged a copy of the blinking pink blob over to the nav station.

"Take us into an RSO at these epirefs, Mr Kurita."

"Reference Stationary Orbit at surface coordinates, aye, sir."

*

Two months earlier, after *The Morrigan* had been snatched away from the weapons of the Faker's Head navy, the surge from the ship's reactor had continued to build. Anne Goldeneyed sat in the captain's chair calling for reports and issuing orders, but the total output from the power plant was being diverted away from the onboard systems. She and the crew became helpless passengers in their own vessel.

Internal and external sensors were all dead, and without telemetry there was no way of telling the destination of the crumple, or how long the journey would take. It was at that point that basic life-support went off line.

The three ships, the *Epona*, the *Hecate* and the *The Morrigan*, had come under outside control. Anne knew, by the constant pricking of her skin, that her ship had been hijacked by the alien artefact. She had no idea how it was doing it, or indeed even what it was that it was doing, but she reasoned that it had got them away from torpedo-based death.

She also had a sly suspicion as to where it was that the wand was taking them. If her hunch proved correct, then she was about to find the world of cinnabar recorded on the treasure map.

After twelve hours without environmental systems, the air temperature dropped below freezing. Anne was finally forced to give in to bioform necessity; there was no way that she or the other living members of the crew could survive without life support. Reluctantly she gave the order to go to stasis.

As Mr Kurita and the Blain twins brought *The Morrigan* closer to the world of Little Bear, Anne watched its approaching bulk, her eyes without focus, the corner of her lower lip wedged under her right canine tooth. A mere two months in the crumple, and they had covered a distance that not even the top grade military ships of the Ancorp navy could have managed.

As they moved into a low orbit, all stealth systems engaged, Anne gave the order for the *Epona* and the *Hecate* to separate. The smaller ships undocked to take up picket defence positions.

In the years since the wand had come into her possession, Anne had said nothing about the artefact to any of her crew. The vast opencast mine that it showed, and the unimaginable wealth of cinnabar, had been her secret and hers alone. She considered that the trail of blood that led finally to her hands made it safer that way. She knew that she would have to tell them soon, but not yet, she decided, not yet.

As *The Morrigan* slid into her RSO over Little Bear, Anne personally took the job of scanning the planet's surface. As a pretext to move Philip Blain away from tactical, she ordered him to do a complete systems check of *The Morrigan*, sliding herself into his chair almost before he was out of it.

Within a few minutes, she had scanned the planet's surface below and found the colony buildings, or more accurately, what remained of them. A series of rectilinear structures marked out what could have been roadways or walls of buildings. Interspersed here and there were the circular shadows of old style Terran control domes, laid out on the sand like a map of some ancient Ozymandiville.

As she increased the resolution, she was able to see that some of the buildings still stood but most were nothing but burnt-out walls and rubble. However, the wreckage of some failed Terran colony was hardly what Anne Goldeneyed was interested in.

The alien wand in her cabin had been traded for life after life, until it had come into her possession. The cinnabar it displayed had been the bait that had taken Anne, and all those hapless others before her, sharpening their appetite for riches. Yet, since going into stasis two months before, she had covered over forty light-years. Now that, she thought, was a secret worth having, a secret that was potentially worth more than all the cinnabar in all the worlds of the human realm put together.

If she were to find it, she needed to look, not in the vast excavation that the wand promised, but in the abandoned city and its ghostly forest of alien towers.

For the next thirty-six hours, Anne mapped, probed and analysed the surface from orbit. She stayed on the bridge not taking a break. Hypothalamic nanobots, set to release Rexin-O, kept her awake and focused. Scan after scan of the planet, in every range, all came back blank. No city, no mine, and not a hint that either had ever existed. All that her instruments showed was featureless desert.

She began to wonder again about the age of the wand. Suppose, she thought, that it was several thousand years old. The city could be nothing but sand under dunes of more sand. The mine, filled in and impossible to find, at least not with *The Morrigan*'s basic commercial sensor suite.

It was possible, she thought, that the wand was a relic of a culture that became extinct uncounted millennia before.

Anne pored over the data. She went through every submenu and setting, refining and changing and rescanning, and the result was always the same: nothing. There was nothing there.

The only thing that showed on her sensors was the broken remains of where the colonists had settled. No signs of life came from the planet at all - no energy signatures from generators, no RF either in the ranges used by bioforms or on the internal range available for PCDs, nothing thermal, passage and presence detectors all flat-lining. A dead colony on a dead world.

After a day and a half in the chair she finally reached the inevitable conclusion.

"Warm up the *Raven*," she ordered Mr Kurita, "and prepare the drop-squad. I'm going to the surface."

Anne's reasoning was straightforward: planet of origin for alien wand and incalculable wealth, and a destroyed human settlement … coincidence?

If there were any clues on the surface that were not visible to her orbital observation techniques, the best place to start looking for them would be down amongst the ruins planetside.

She made her way to the hangar at the base of the command spire of *The Morrigan* to begin the pre-flights for the first of her ships.

The *Raven* was the vessel that she had taken all those years ago on New Skye. This old and battered shuttle had a very special place in the affections of Anne Gold-eneyed. It had lifted her from her slavery, and set her amongst the stars.

She palmed the hatch and let herself into the cold, dark interior. The arctic air of the ship pinched her nostrils, making her eyes sting, and her breath became a frozen plume as she walked down the cramped central corridor to the cockpit, her boots clanking on the deck grating. She had to duck a couple of times to avoid the pipes of the airflow system, and every surface was covered in the rime of open space.

The hatch to the flight deck stuttered for a second as the frozen mechanism tried to overcome the ice, but with a creak it broke free and slid away. The cabin lights came up in a weak greeting and Anne took her accustomed seat. She could feel the damp and icy surface of the pilot's bucket through the leather of her trousers, frosty against the skin of her thighs, the cold of space making the chair slippery and unyielding.

A ship as old as the *Raven* could not simply be started up like some sportster straight from the chandler's yard; she required understanding, and coaxing, and the patience that mechanisms need as they become decrepit in unique ways. If anyone other than Anne tried to bring the *Raven* to readiness, at best they would merely fail, at worst they could either release a burst of lethal radiation, or detonate the main plasma ring in a high yield thermonuclear blast.

The shuttle woke under Anne's affectionate touch the way an ancient cat does when stroked before a fire - bit by bit, and without hurry. She heard the O-units sigh as atmospherics came online. She felt a distant lurch as the onboard artificial gravity took over from that of *The Morrigan*. Suddenly the starboard side of the ship was slightly uphill, where the gravity grids needed recalibration.

One of the plasma induction constrictors around the ring would occasionally stick in the 'on' position, so she dry-initiated three or four times to make sure it was moving freely. Fuel storage indicated half capacity, which was more than enough for a simple down-and-up.

The view from the front of the ship showed the white of the ice-coated hangar walls suddenly burst into dazzling brilliance as the external lights came up. Through the decking she felt the mechanical vibrations of *The Morrigan*'s cranes as they powered up in order to swing the Blain twins into position.

Richard and Philip Blain were the only bioform humans Anne allowed on *The Morrigan*. The twins had been the result of an illegal clone purchase on planet Casablanca. A local Ancorp commissar had, in the name of defence, beefed up the Homeworld Security Force to keep a tighter reign on the sizeable immigrant population of North Australs, refugees from the long running civil war. The Blain twins had been part of those measures, genetically manipulated and tricked out with a full set of military grade implants.

Anne had seen the twins often enough as she moved in and out of Casablancan territorial space. Fortunately, for a wandering smuggler like her, they were amenable to reasonable bribery.

For all their phenomenal dogfight prowess, it became apparent to Anne over the few months that she was running refugees into the system, that what the Blain twins really yearned for was escape.

Very specifically, to escape the monastic confines of a single-sex clone barracks, and to get away to a planet where the concept of "girl-friend" could be made a flesh and blood reality.

Casablanca had been settled by a stern sect of sin believers known as the Conclave of Transgressors, and the clone brothers had been kept in a single sex military academy, force fed a diet of religious and political propaganda. The rest of the vat born warriors in the barracks had been created for the system and knew no other way of being, but the Blain twins were an exception. They had been custom made at Geneflexion Station for a different conflict, and were already fourteen years old when the Commissar had bought them as ex-rentals.

Five years later when Anne had come across them, as an escaped slave herself, she knew that they were ripe for the picking. She was not able to offer them much, other than freedom and the promise of epigenetic reprogramming, but the deal clincher for the boys had been access to the fleshpots of dozens of new worlds. The thought of a biologically based lifestyle had been enough for the twins. Freedom was nothing without pleasure.

They had escaped one night when on patrol in a couple of Corvus D-65 fighters, which were now in the process of being attached to the outside of the *Raven*'s hull.

The symmetrical diamonds of the D-65s extended on the boom arms of the hangar cranes, PCD crews waving the fighters into position and securing them to the hull attachments.

Anne looked back along the *Raven* and saw into the cockpits of the fighters. Each of the Blain twins gave her a thumbs-up, and she showed blues across the board. From behind her in the crew compartment, she heard the clatter and shouts of her squad of PCDs as they stowed themselves in the drop chutes.

A blast of reasonably warm air finally emerged from the heater, and she moved the pilot's bucket forward into the flight position. She felt completely at home here, surrounded by her ship, part of it.

"Open the hangar," she ordered. The decompression alert klaxons began to blare out, and the PCD crews unhurriedly left the launch bay as the massive outer door slid back. The atmospheric restraining field changed from red to blue, and the gravity grids went offline. The launch clamps released and the *Raven* was free. Anne eased her hands into the interface and felt her ship respond to her. Beyond the hangar the surface of Little Bear filled her sight. She closed her eyes and willed the *Raven* forward.

As she looked down over the planet, there were no clouds, nothing between her and its arid surface. So the turbulence that took the old shuttle as it completed atmospheric insertion surprised her with its violence. However once she dropped out of the undetected jet stream, into the quieter air of the lower atmosphere, she was able to initiate aerodynamic flight model.

She gave the Blain twins the order to launch, and the two bat-wing fighters separated and took up escort position. The feed from the sensor systems aboard *The Morrigan* had been patched through to her, and a pink blob marking the position of the wrecked colony blinked on the horizon ahead.

As she surveyed the ancient and desolate sands, she finally saw in a way that she could believe that there was nothing on the surface to indicate any life had ever existed here, let alone something that had been capable of building the city from the wand.

The *Raven* and the two fighters soared high above the desert, homing in on the epirefs of the destroyed colony buildings. By the time she had a visual on the site, she was convinced that there was nothing here worth finding. The planet was a bust, which left her with a far more serious problem of how to get back to anywhere civilised.

She banked the *Raven* hard over and circled the central colony compound twice, looking for a good spot to set down. The main admin tower seemed to be intact, and one of the larger control domes looked like a promising place to have a poke around.

"Caution! This vessel is landing. Please look up. Caution! This vessel…" The standard health and safety warning and accompanying high pitched siren competed with the roar of the manoeuvring thrusters, announcing the *Raven's* arrival to the ghosts of Little Bear as Anne set down.

Taitere

Anne Goldeneyed stood in the charcoal shadow of what had once been a generator hut. On the blackened sand before her, Sergeant Huehnergard examined the access panels on the chassis of an old style PCD that they had found amongst the ruins of Little Bear.

"I never know whether these things are screwed down or just clipped on," he said, as much to himself as to Anne. "And if I tug at stuff until it comes off, I usually break it."

"Do you think you can revive it?" she asked. The old arteform soldier was crouched down over the weird looking frame.

"Judging by all the arms, that and the ugly chrome job, it probably dates from the second half of the last century," he said by way of an answer.

"Was that a yes or a no?"

"That was a 'I don't know 'til I try little girl', but if you keep bugging me I may forget something important in a long chain of complicated steps and totally destroy anything that I might otherwise be able to salvage. Do you want to go away and have a little walk around now, *keptin*?"

If anybody else spoke to Anne in this way then they were looking to book a short flight out of the nearest airlock. However the sergeant was a special case. It had been Huehnergard that had saved her life all those years ago on New Skye, and without him, she would never have made it off planet.

The thirteen-year-old Anne, already on the run for the murders involved with her escape, found him where they had him stored, in one of the warehouses near the plantation's up-strip. He was lying in a coffin-shaped pakenstak, deactivated and ready to be wiped.

Sergeant Huehnergard had been bought in with simple low-level building security in mind, and a reconditioned soldier PCD like the Sarge was all that the job needed. He was delivered to the compound after a lifetime of frontline service in the innumerable skirmishes of the Corporate Federation, and immediately failed the initial diagnostic tests.

He told Anne later that they had found multiple cross-linked errors between memory and personality systems, and as he was still under guarantee, they deactivated him until gang-master Templeman could get around to wiping his core. The House Fathers of Skye arranged for a replacement personality to be shipped to them.

The frightened little girl, hiding in the dark of the plantation's warehouse, had imprinted the sergeant when she found him. He was cold and stripped of weaponry. Her pale hands frozen, trembling and stained for the first time with human blood, the young runaway, had re-powered the dormant PCD, knifing his command registry and writing herself in as his Bioform-in-Charge.

In the dark and against the sound of the screaming mud-bear pack closing on her scent, she had called him back to life to serve as her protector, a rôle he took to with software-based dedication. He became her hollow knight, despatching her problems with predatory efficiency.

Had he wanted to, the sergeant could have undone Anne's ham-fisted reprogramming in a New York Nano, but he had a Bioform-in-Charge now, a reason to live, and he knew better than to question that.

The ensuing murderous chase across New Skye lasted nearly a standard month before Anne and the Sarge, as she now called him, managed to slip undetected onto an upship to the orbital scrapyard. The two of them had purloined the *Raven* from the carcass of one of the great liners that came to New Skye to die a piece at a time in the cold heavens above the planet.

The condemned trio, Anne Goldeneyed, Sergeant Huehnergard and the *Raven*, escaped New Skye attached to the hull of a passing ore freighter bound for the mines of planet Salisbury. For Anne it was the start of her free life.

Due to his system errors, the sergeant could be somewhat vague at times, and over the years Anne had learned to make certain allowances for her saviour, yet there was a bond between them that ran deeper than flesh and metal. Anne smiled to herself and turned, leaving the sergeant to get on with reviving the PCD.

The landing party from *The Morrigan* had been dirt-side for nearly the whole of one sun-scorched local day. She was beginning to wonder why these people from Earth could ever have chosen a planet like this. The heat and the smell were incredible.

The wrecked buildings were clearly those of a scientific outpost. Anne thought it was more likely to be a pre-colony evaluation mission rather than a full-blown terraforming operation. However, this was only a guess based on the number and shape of the structures. There was no documentation to be found anywhere around the base, anything that could have any stored records had been removed. Each and every structure had been methodically stripped down to the walls before they were burned. There was nothing in the wreckage except rubble.

Of the colonists, there was no clue as to their fate. Anne would have liked some biological remains, a corpse or two, something which would have given her some data as to how long ago whatever catastrophe it was that befell the settlement happened.

She stood for a second in the middle of a sand-covered roadway, one arm raised to shield her eyes against the glare of the star. Broken towers and the cracked eggshells of control domes surrounded her, casting their fuzzy shadows onto the skin of this silent world. The wand had brought her here. This planet wanted her here.

"Talk to me," she whispered to the ruins.

The PCD frame that the Sarge worked to revive seemed to have been deliberately hidden under a tarpaulin in the generator hut after it had been gutted by fire. Deactivated, it had lain where it had obviously been carefully placed, powered down and dead. Even the hand-held scanners of the drop squad had not detected it. It had only been found when Anne had ordered a visual survey of the entire ruin.

Philip Blain approached from one of the ruined buildings. He was flanked by a pair of armed PCDs. Anne found her gaze lingering over the young man. Blond hair and cold eyes, the length of his legs emphasized by the ugly scatter blaster in a thigh holster. Occasionally she would catch sight of a Blain twin from the corner of her eye, and sometimes she was surprised by her own reactions.

A depressed sigh escaped her lips and she crossed her arms across her chest.

"Anything at all?" she called out as he drew near.

"Sand and rubble, stink and heat, and any number of other good reasons to leave, but nothing to say what happened here."

"Little girl, you may want to get here. Like now, you know." The sergeant's voice whispered into her implants. She waved for the Blain to follow her, and turned and went back to the generator hut.

The silver arteform was backed into a corner, the ends of two of its arms sparking like cattle-prods.

"I want to see a bioform. I want to see a bioform," he was repeating, waving the tazer arms around until Anne walked in through the gap that used to be a door.

"Show me your skin," the arteform shouted.

"You screwed up the activation sequence," Anne said flatly to the sergeant.

"No, this one is a sane as it ever was."

"Show me your skin," shouted the arteform again.

"Nah," said Anne, thinking aloud. "Kill it."

"No, wait. I have to know if you are infected."

The voice from the arteform was suddenly calm.

"Infected?" Anne was just about to turn and leave the hut, but the question brought her up short.

"Infected with what? Is that what happened here, everyone killed by a plague?"

"Not killed, worse. Please show me your skin. I have to know that you are clear before I can open my log files to you."

The PCD floated very slowly towards Anne, taking one of her hands in two of his own like a guilty lover's reassurance.

She did not resist, gaining confidence from the smooth click of Philip Blain's well maintained scatter blaster being cocked just behind her. The PCD brought another two of its arms around and, very slowly, so as not to startle the bioform holding the weapon, it rolled back her sleeve revealing the skin of her forearm.

"The infection causes external tracks of pseudo-nerve tissue to develop. Parasitic dendrites which allow for the transport of alien neurotransmitters. They tap in to the victim's own nervous system, overriding the host organism's brain chemistry and hijacking the infected creature. You are clear, no tracks means no infection."

The PCD backed away a little.

"We have to get word to Earth," he said. "It took them all. The infection took them all, and those it couldn't infect it killed."

"Infection? What infection?" whispered Anne.

"It was unlike anything we had ever seen. It's an intelligent disease," answered the PCD. "And it has learned how to take humans."

A bioform male materialised without warning in the middle of the area enclosed by the burned-out walls. Anne felt herself roughly pushed out of the way and, without her knowing how he had done it, Philip Blain stood in front of her, his scatter blaster levelled at the man's chest.

"Calm down, vat-boy," said Sergeant Huehnergard. "It's just a 3v. You should maybe consider a refund on those implants of yours."

Anne saw the end of the Blain twin's scatter blaster swing around toward the Sarge. She sucked her teeth loudly, and Philip caught the look in her eye. He lowered the weapon.

"I am Specialist Ulysses Grainger of the Ancorp Planetary Survey, assigned to the Mercator," began the image that the PCD was projecting. "I am the last survivor of the Ten Suns mission."

The image of Specialist Grainger was tall and burly. He was mousey blond with an ill-kept beard. His expedition uniform was ripped and stained.

"If you are watching this then I am already dead."

The striking green eyes of Specialist Grainger briefly lit with a spark of dark humour.

"You know, that really was in my top-ten list of things that I hoped I'd never have to say. It was right up there with 'Ramming speed'." He allowed himself a brief gallows chuckle.

"We arrived on Little Bear about eighteen standard months ago, towards the end of 73FR."

Anne turned to Philip Blain. "What year is it now?" Philip shrugged.

"How am I supposed to know? I have two times, day-time or night-time, and I'm not always sure about those."

"He recorded this sometime in 75FR, how long ago was that? Sarge?"

"You have been in stasis seven times since the last time I was able to update my clock, but adding all stasis time to last known good, I make it somewhere around 175 FR plus or minus two or three years for drift."

Anne looked stunned.

"You mean I'm more than eighty years old?"

"For the first year it all went really well." Specialist Grainger carried on regardless. "Planet Little Bear doesn't look such a good prospect from space, until you get close up to it. But once you do, Little Bear is suitable for one-hundred percent terraforming. That how she got her name, 'cause like baby bear in the Three Bears, everything she had was 'just right'.

"We couldn't figure out how a barren world like this one could have such a significant percentage of oxygen in its atmosphere, but to be honest, we weren't overly bothered where it came from. As it turned out, we really should have been."

The figure of Specialist Grainger sat down on the sand.

"Oxygen is produced by life. Little Bear is inhabited, or at least was.

"The first two victims were Specialists Wheeler and Gorana. They discovered the city on the Kiengi Plains, about three-hundred kilometres from here. They were gone for two weeks. We searched for days, but found nothing, no wreckage, no bodies. We thought they were dead.

"If this message ever gets back to Earth, when whoever you are sees this, these people will be just names off the manifest - Wheeler, Gorana, Grainger - but these were real lives in real flesh, my friends. Specialist Gorana and I were at school on the Chandos facility. He was in the same class as my brother, and I remember him as a sixteen-year-old. He came to stay with us one time, and all the luggage he brought with him was a grav-board and a tooth kit.

"Specialist Wheeler and I met at college. We used to get drunk at the same rate, which meant we always had someone that we could talk to. So when I thought they were dead, I hadn't lost a couple of names off the crew roster, I had lost a part of my own life.

"Then they came back. Simple as that, they walked out of the desert, saying that they had found the ruins of some alien city. What I didn't know, what nobody knew, was that they were already dead inside. The infection had taken them, they were just infected shells, husks, doing the bidding of the alien contamination, and I didn't see it, nobody did, not until it was too late. Professor van der Putt, the expedition leader, went to explore the site, and after a few days we got the order to move the entire expedition to the alien city.

"I flew a couple of shuttle trips to the city and back, but some of the others started acting strange. And then some started not to come back."

Specialist Grainger reached into his overalls and produced a pack of cigarettes.

"Doc McMurdo caught me as I was helping load another shuttle dash. I thought he was going a bit strange. He ripped open my uniform to get a look at my chest. I know why now, but when he did it, it cost him a smack in the mouth.

"He'd found out about the infection and managed to knock out a couple of the infectees. He was babbling on about skin contact and long chain molecules, and mitochondrial DNA. I'm a cartographer, not my field this stuff, but I got a copy of his files, and Albert, this PCD, has everything stored away in his personality core.

"The only thing I can do is try and get the Mercator off and away, get back to Earth, or anywhere with a transmitter. Everyone is gone, the PCDs have no choice but to serve their infected masters. Albert and I are the last ones left, and I have to leave him here in case I don't make it.

"If you are watching this where you found Albert here, I have only one piece of advice. Leave. Leave now. Get off world, and if you have the means, core-crack the planet. If this infection spreads it's the end for us."

"Speak for yourself, fleshy," added Sergeant Huehnergard cheerfully. Anne casually clipped him around the back of his head. Specialist Grainger faded from existence.

"Did he make it, Albert?" she asked.

In reply the spidery-looking PCD pointed at what Anne had thought was the main slab of the admin tower. The top section was missing, and the edges of what was left showed the unmistakable signs of a large explosion.

"That's the Mercator."

"Oké," snapped Anne, clapping her hands together and turning to leave. "Sarge, contact the rest of the drop squad, and get back to the *Raven*.

"Philip, find your brother and get ready for air-docking. We are leaving. Anybody not back at the ship by the time we're ready to lift gets left. RF that out, Sarge".

"What about me?" the question came from Albert.

"Sarge, deactivate that, will you? That is the ugliest frame I have ever seen, and I won't have it on my ship."

"No wait…" Whatever arguments Albert was about to put disappeared with a click as the sergeant deactivated him. The PCD fell to the sand, just so much metal. Anne looked at it briefly and remembered another deactivated PCD, left to die in the cold and dark.

"Bring his personality core with us. We'll see if we can find a better frame for him somewhere, shall we, Sarge?"

"Thank you, little girl. I was going to do it anyway, but now it doesn't have to be a secret."

"Come on, come on, come on," said Anne hustling back towards the *Raven*. "Let's blow this ball."

"I hear that," said the Sarge.

Anne had the *Raven* ready to lift within ten minutes of deciding it was time for the up. Despite her threat to leave any stragglers on the sand, she sat with the engine running, waiting for the furthest members of her squad to return to the LZ for dust-off. Only when the last of them was safely installed in their drop tubes did she engage the fluidic injectors and release her grip on the world of Little Bear.

The heavy old bird tore into the heavens under full thrust, leaving a column of boiling air behind her that twisted like a hazy tornado. Slowing, and levelling off at three-thousand meters, Anne began a sweep out to the west of the expedition site, heading towards the rendezvous with the Blain twins. She opened a channel to Nancy Kurita aboard *The Morrigan*.

"Prep the docking bay," she barked, shouting to be heard over the screaming turbines. "We're on our way back."

"What happened down there?"

"Not now, Nancy. I'm sort of concentrating on getting my clones and my fighters back. Oké with you?" She closed the channel without waiting for a reply.

Ahead of her, high above the desert sands, Anne saw the super-cruise steam trails the D-65s were leaving as feathery white tracks across the sulphurous sky. She opened the makeshift docking clamps, lashed-up to allow the shuttle to act as a split-ship. Then, setting the nose straight and level, she set to docking speed. When it came to docking manoeuvres there was nothing more she needed to do, everything else was up to the enhanced skills of the twins.

First one, then the other Blain dropped into formation beside her. She checked their position and was about to give the order to dock when her entire skin suddenly began to tingle like the static build up just before a lightning strike.

The overwhelming feeling broke over her, shocking and cold as a bucket of thrown ice water. She yelped loudly in sudden outrage. It felt as sharp as if she had unexpectedly sat on a caterprickle.

The *Raven* had flown into some kind of projected field that felt similar to when she handled the wand, yet vastly more powerful. Every nerve in her body resonated with interferential energy. It was as if alien fingers were reaching under her skin and raking their nails over her internal organs.

She could hear the air around her crackling, and every square centimetre of her skin was being stabbed with invisible needles. Components in her console sparked and fused together with little puffs of smoke.

She yelped in panic as she realised that the flight systems were going offline. The reactor plasma quietly collapsed, and the twin turbines slowly fell silent. Anne was plunged into eerie quiet. Nothing except for the whistle of the air over the stumpy wings and the creaks and groans of the airframe. The *Raven* was going down.

Anne had a few seconds to activate the dead-stick systems. Her interface with the *Raven* suddenly cut, her only remaining control being the two emergency joysticks that allowed her direct access to the control planes of the aerodynamic flight system.

The B.A.B.D. Systems model 40 shuttle had never been designed with any glide capability in mind, and without power, the *Raven* pitched forward. Anne leaned back in the pilot's bucket, her entire bodyweight pulling back on the sticks like a rower leaning into the oars, trying to get the *Raven* to flare. After what seemed an eternity, the foreshortened control surfaces bit into the airflow and the nose of the *Raven* lifted marginally above the horizon.

From the corner of her eye, she caught sight of one of the Blain twins. The fighter was in the same situation as her. The familiar steam trail of the super-cruise engine had puffed out, and the aircraft was now nothing more than a giant arrowhead pointed at the planet.

The prickling sensation in her skin became even more intense. Grimly she held on to the sticks, trying to keep the airframe at a stable angle. She realised there was not even power for the docking suspensors. This was going to be a belly landing.

As she wrestled with the falling ship, an inky circle bruised the sky ahead of her. The swirling dark area resembled the crumple summoned by the wand back at the Faker's Head system. From its edges a graduated rainbow of shimmering darkness spread across the yellow sky. Anne, struggling with the controls, was unable to make out what she was looking at. Suddenly, the core of darkness that had formed solid as a stone exploded. A black wave surged across the sky, blocking out the light from the star.

The darkness had a tangible fabric. It enveloped the *Raven* as if the plummeting bird had flown into a velvet cloud shot through with purple lightning. Anne had no idea what was happening, other than her immediate problems of keeping the *Raven* on an even keel.

Her ship was dead, the stubby wings making only marginal difference between gliding and falling. She was not even sure that the dead stick systems were having any effect at all. The *Raven* seemed to be making its own course corrections. Anne was losing height rapidly. She was down to less than five hundred meters. Desperately she tried to sweep the ship around in a series of 'S' shaped manoeuvres to bleed the speed off, but she was too low and too fast. Then, in a flash of purple lightning, she saw what she had come here to find, and what she now sought to escape.

The abandoned city of the wand, like the projection in her cabin, was edging its way into the universe, its buildings appearing as transparent projections, becoming more solid as she flew towards them. Anne, wide-eyed as a frightened child, tried to understand what she was seeing. The city was materialising before her as if summoned by an ancient and dark magic.

Ahead of her a massive, slab sided building loomed vast above the skyline of the city. She leaned the shuttle hard over, trying to avoid the immense obstacle, but the *Raven* no longer responded to even the limited controls of the emergency flight systems.

With no time to imagine the terrible forces of the crash, Anne saw the building as the fly sees the swatter, without visualising what would happen next. She was still pulling back vainly on the sticks as, with a scream of fury and frustration, she smashed into the side of the organic looking tower.

Maitere

Anne saw the nose of the *Raven* touch the skin of the edifice in a moment of non-time that was almost a kiss between the bird and the building. Then with a deafening roar of reality, time avalanched, compressed into an incomprehensible blur as the moment caught up with itself, and the shuttle exploded through the alien wall.

The shell of the building was without structure, merely a fragile organic crust a couple of meters thick, and the tower nothing but a hollow chimney. She sliced through the insubstantial fabric of the building as if it were made of dried sea-foam, bursting in from the outside. Debris and billowing dust from the impact hung seemingly motionless, like a horizontal mushroom-cloud. It froze the scene for a Nano into a static tableau of balanced forces.

Robbed of her momentum, gravity turned the *Raven*'s nose towards the ground and Anne felt herself thrown against the webbing of her seat harness as she fell. She took and held an involuntary breath as the nose of the shuttle drooped like a roller coaster going over the first rise. The ship was now pointed directly at the heart of the world.

Suddenly, blue light surrounded her. Rows of dark sapphire beams burst into life from unseen projectors that lined the length of the shaft. They filled the core of the tower with a scintillating web of force-lines. Before she had a chance to fall further, the *Raven* was caught fast, as if in a cerulean gel.

Her ship was held nose down, suspended in, and surrounded by, this eerie field that was more darkness than light. The beams were accompanied by an intense but low-pitched hum, and the pricking of her skin became synchronised with the modulation of this deep, orchestral booming bass note.

Rotating slowly clockwise, the shuttle was brought back to its normal orientation, and passed unhurriedly and smoothly down between the beams, held captive, until she was placed, quite gently, on the ground.

Bewildered, Anne sat shocked and breathless for a few moments. The only sound was the overpowering drone of the tractor field generators, a gothic organ swell that shook her whole world. She looked around in the darkness, wondering what would happen next.

As if waking, her mental focus returned and she became reconnected to events, realising that action had again become possible. She forced herself to release her corpse-like grip on the flight sticks, shrugged off her seat webbing, staggered up from the pilot's bucket and ripped open the weapons locker behind her, urgently grabbing the scatter blaster and plastol from within. With trembling hands, she fumbled with the old-fashioned buckle on her holster as she strapped the handgun to her thigh, slinging the blaster over her shoulder. From the crash-kit, she grabbed a torch and the emergency crank for the drop tubes.

Anne forced open the door to the cabin and went back into the darkness of the main hold, and with some effort turned the crank-handle to open the first tube. The Sarge lay on his drop-frame, all status displays indicating he was dead.

Whatever had knocked out all power on the *Raven* had also apparently killed her PCDs. Anne sat down heavily on the decking of the central gangway. Sergeant Huehnergard was about the nearest thing that she had to an actual friend.

The blue light that spilled into the ship from outside abruptly ceased, and as it did so the prickling of her skin also stopped. The foghorn bass note that accompanied the light faded away with the persistence of a sustain pedal.

The silence was now complete and perfect. It made a deep emptiness in her stomach. She looked around and realised that she was completely alone, and for the first time in her adult life she understood the full weight of the word 'helpless'.

There was a loud click, the internal power relays tripped, and the cold blue of the emergency lighting came up through the ship. As she watched, the small status display on the front of Sergeant Huehnergard's chassis began to flash and the PCD frame initiated its start sequence. Anne sniffed hard, wiping the end of her nose with the back of her hand and waited. Thirty seconds later the sergeant spoke.

"Fifty years since I had a cigarette, and the first thought through my mind every time I wake is 'God! I'd love a smoke.'"

"Welcome back, Sarge." The relief in her voice was deep and heartfelt.

"Back?" He sounded puzzled. "Have I been somewhere?"

With some difficulty and not much grace, the Sarge began to pull himself free of the drop-frame. Muffled shouts and bangs could be heard from the other tubes as the PCDs reactivated.

"Never mind," said Anne as she stood. "We have more urgent problems."

She turned and ran back to the cockpit.

"Get the rest of the squad ready for defensive deployment," she ordered over her shoulder.

With the back-up power restored, Anne's first reaction was to see if she could re-initialise the plasma reactor. She threw herself into the pilot's bucket and went through start-up. Her fingers still shook and her ears were full of the sound of her own breathless panting but she could see that she made no mistakes as she ran through the sequence. The reactor refused to fire up.

Anne was still trying to figure this out when the belly ramp of the shuttle opened, and, under the supervision of Sgt Huehnergard, the drop squad took up positions on the grey and dusty surface, creating a defensive perimeter.

A notch of brilliant daylight appeared as the wall directly ahead of her cockpit split open in an uncomfortably organic way. Standing silhouetted against the brightness was a single human figure. Without hurry, the figure began walking towards the ship.

Anne was still wrapped up trying to get the *Raven* to kick over. She could hear Sgt Huehnergard shouting instructions and warnings, but his voice was little more than a vague distraction. It was only when she heard the words "halt or I fire" that she realised the importance of what was happening outside. She leapt up and flew from the cockpit. Racing down the centre corridor, she jumped the ladder into the hold and down the ramp.

"Stand down, Sarge," she shouted.

"Aye, sir," he said, lowering the aim of his weapons.

The human figure continued to approach, until it came into range of the lights of the *Raven*. One of the armed PCDs stopped the stranger with a hand placed on his chest. He halted ten metres from where Anne stood. She could see that he was a small blond man in his late twenties, dressed in a loose boiler suit. As he stood in the circle of light that spilled from the ship, she could see that his thin face was covered in almost Maori-like tattoos.

"You are welcome here, Captain Goldeneyed," he called out. "We have anticipated your arrival for some time."

His gaze never engaged with hers, his eyes were without focus.

"We can deal with the niceties after you tell me where my other two crew members are," she said, her voice sharp and her hand resting on the butt of her plastol.

This little man represented whatever force it was that had just brought down her ship and smashed her through the wall of some organic alien cooling tower.

"The vehicles that accompanied you were captured safely, and their pilots are even now being gathered."

The young man suddenly snapped his gaze up to meet Anne's, and there was an inexplicable expression on his face. She had no idea how to interpret the intensity of this stare.

"There is transport. You are also to be gathered. Follow."

The young man did not wait for an answer. He turned and began to walk back to the door of the structure. Anne turned to the sergeant.

"You and one other with me, the rest to guard the ship. Ten seconds."

With that she started after the retreating figure. Exactly ten seconds later she was joined by Sergeant Huehnergard and another PCD that she recognised as Eddie.

"All safeties off," she said quietly. "All that stuff over his face, he's gotta be infected, so if there's gonna be any accidents make sure they happen to him, Oké? I don't want this freak-boy getting close to me, understood?"

"Yes, sir," the two PCDs answered in unison.

"Oké Sarge, Eddie, update mission profile parameter file, ident string 'Anne Goldeneyed of New Skye' Primary: defend me, physical attack. Secondary: retrieve the Blain bioforms where it does not risk compromising primary mission objective. Update and confirm."

Both the Sarge and Eddie updated their mission parameter files and confirmed.

Anne's voice dropped in both pitch and volume.

"I want my boys back, but I won't die for it, you got that?"

Anne reached the door and stepped outside to be hit by the heat. She squinted, shading her eyes with her hand, trying to adjust to the fearsome daylight. The storm of blackness that had overpowered the *Raven* had evaporated, leaving a bright and clear yellow sky.

Near the base of the tower was a small orange vehicle. It had three wheels with balloon tyres; the back was open and consisted of two benches. The young man had stepped into the bubble-shaped cabin, and she was obviously expected to ride in the back. The whole impression that the vehicle gave was one of cheap and unpleasant utility.

"We'll follow you," shouted Anne at the driver. "I'm not getting in that," she whispered to herself. "Looks like a sewer wagon."

Sergeant Huehnergard extended a pillion at the back of his frame and Anne mounted up, holding onto his shoulders. The young man set off, Anne and the sergeant following on at the buggy's maximum speed of forty kilometres per hour.

Little Bear barged uninvited into Anne's world of frantic analysis and speculation, destroying her chain of thought with its solid reality. The focus of her gaze suddenly widened out from the buggy, and she realised the extent of her outsideness. A space farer's life was a claustrophobic one; its events all taking place in small, manufactured environments. The great nothing of space never gave any real sense of scale, not the same way that this towering city, under the vast dome of inhospitable gold, did.

Before Little Bear, Anne had not been out in an unprotected environment for over a year of waking days, not counting stasis. She could feel the absence of walls. The dry wind felt good through her hair, and the fierce sunlight was already making the skin of her cheeks feel stretched.

She looked around at the spires and walkways of the city, and up at the yellow gold of the sky. These needle-like buildings seemed to have been extruded rather than built, reaching towards the heavens, elegant and alien. Alien, she thought, very definitely alien, in a way that the orange buggy, and the young man that was driving it, equally definitely were not.

Anne remembered Specialist Grainger. It had been over a century since the Earth people had been infected, but the young man in the buggy was clearly less than a hundred years old, therefore, Anne reasoned, the contaminated expedition personnel had been able to breed, each subsequent generation becoming polluted with the alien organism.

She reckoned that with the hundreds of personnel of a full scale planetography team to play with, after a century there could be thousands of them.

The city that she saw as they passed through it was every bit as abandoned as the recording in the wand had suggested. The function of these structures could only be guessed at, but they all had one thing in common. They were empty, desolate and dead. That, and the fact that half an hour ago they had not been here.

"What's going on here, Sarge?" She leaked the question rather than asking it.

"No point asking me, this is bioform stuff."

"Hmmm," said Anne. "Keep your optics open and your weapons on preheat. I need to blow this rock, so I want you ready if it all kicks off."

"No worries, little girl."

The desert had invaded the city so that the buildings rose from it like thorns. The buggy bounced and plodded through the fuzzy reddish shadows of the empty metropolis, until it came to a ramp that led up to a raised roadway that stretched between the towers. Suspensor units activated, and the wheels folded back. The little vehicle now derived its motive power from the road. As it picked up speed, the sergeant and Eddie easily kept pace.

The city was huge. Densely packed buildings marched off to the horizon like an abandoned army. The roadway curved between the towers, and rose and fell as it wound around and over the perfectly preserved buildings. The emptiness of her surroundings suddenly clarified an impression which had until that moment floated just out of her grasp.

This city was empty, yes, but it was not a ruin. Everything that had been built here had not decayed one iota since the day that it had been left. Not abandoned, but abiding. The spires waited for something. As she made this realisation, and despite the heat of the day, Anne felt a chill run down her spine, the gooseflesh rising on her arms. There was something ghostly in these black towers, something intelligent and malevolent in the structures themselves.

Ahead of her the roadway began to climb at a steep angle, before a spur of the flyover split away and ran off into one of the towers. She tried unsuccessfully to peer into the darkness of the building. As she turned her attention back to the direction they were travelling, the sergeant came over the rise and she was able to see before her the focus of the city.

The wand had not shown her this. The roadway now travelled between the towers about half a kilometre from the ground, and the view was breathtaking. The city was built around a vast organic looking dome. She could see roads like the one she was on, converging from all points of the city, feeding into the huge, glistening black structure.

This was the nucleus of the metropolis, set within a deep crater-like indentation in the desert. The vast structure resembled the corpse of some monstrous black jellyfish washed up on the sand. Roads and tube-ways penetrated the skin at thousands of points over the surface. Each opening an organic orifice, the skin of the building gathered away from the invading highways with folded ramparts, like the ridges of eyelids.

To Anne the black dome looked like the mouth of a sea-anemone, the roads acting like fronds, wafting morsels of food towards the great black maw. In her mind's eye, it became a many tentacled demon, waiting at the middle of its web, patient as a spider. She was about to lean forward to tell the Sarge to head back to the *Raven* but she caught herself. If she ran away, her ship would still be stuck to the ground. Whatever it was that had disabled the old bird was under that black canopy, as were no doubt the Blain twins.

"Easy girl," she whispered to herself through clenched teeth. "You think too much."

She focused briefly on the orange bubble of the buggy that had been sent for her.

There was nothing demonic about the skinny disease ridden young man and his silly little wagon. She allowed herself to be reassured by its human quality, using it to put the nature of his contagion out of her mind. Contact, Grainger had said. All she had to do was stay out of reach. How hard could that be?

As they rode on, the dome grew until it filled her entire view of the world. She reckoned that the structure must have been tens of kilometres from edge to edge, and maybe three kilometres from the base of the crater to the tip of the dome. Her stomach dropped as their party crossed over what was in effect a moat that surrounded the edifice. The side of the crater below her was smooth, and a manufactured surface - it disappeared into the stygian depths below.

The road was now several hundred meters wide, and the archway that they entered the dome by stretched open with the good intent of a stuffed pike. They whistled into the darkness of the dome, and Anne became aware that the speed that they were travelling at had built to over a hundred kilometres per hour.

The interior was at first total darkness, but as Anne's eyes realised that they were shielded from the blinding intensity of Little Bear's star, they opened up enough to show that here and there were random patterns of lights. She began to get the impression that the city carried on under the dome. The roadway was still travelling between towers and rotundas, but now some of these hung from the ceiling, like stalactites … or teeth.

Ahead and to her right, they passed an obstacle, and beyond it Anne was able to see an area that was bathed in the orange sodium glow of artificial light. The buggy began to slow. A large multi-rotunda tower rose up out of the darkness, and before it was a Kremlin-like collection of mini-domes. Orangey-yellow spotlights created a small umbrella of illumination, lending the tableau the appearance of a snowstorm paperweight.

As they approached Anne could see several more of the buggies, like the one she followed, parked outside what she assumed was the front entrance to the smaller building that they were headed for. A couple of trucks and loaders also stood idle.

The young man drew his vehicle up outside the centre of the domes and emerged from the cab, staring expectantly back at Anne, who with a whispered command of "close enough" ordered the sergeant to pull up, Eddie riding at idle beside her. She dismounted and took a step forward, so that her arteforms were in a defensive position behind her.

"Where are my boys?" she shouted to the young man.

"I am taking you to them," he answered, although his voice was little more than a whisper.

"No," said Anne, drawing her plastol from its holster. "You will have them brought to me."

"A subtle difference, but I feel an important one," muttered the sergeant to himself.

Anne aimed the plastol squarely at the chest of the young man.

"Who are you?"

"I am Kevin," he replied.

"That would usually be a good enough reason to shoot."

"Captain Goldeneyed, your threat behaviour is as useless as it is unnecessary."

This was a new voice. She turned to face the sound. An older man was walking towards her from the shadows. Sergeant Huehnergard turned his headlights onto the man.

"Hold it right there," said Anne, swinging the aim of her plastol around. He stopped, and she was able to get a good look at him. He was thin, and his face had the same tattoo-like swirling tracks as the younger man. He was very fit looking and around sixty. His full head of grey hair was neatly combed and parted down one side. She was also able to see the same curious lack of focus in his face as she had noticed with the other. Most importantly, his hands were empty.

"All I want is my crew members back, and then we will leave you to whatever weird scene you've got going here, and you will never see us again," she said. She realised as she heard the words that it was true. Whatever gains she had thought to get out of this place were not worth whatever it had cost these two freaks.

"You were invited, and you have carried the heart back to the body. Your rôle is finished. We have no concern for what you want."

As soon as he had spoken these words, Anne heard two metallic thuds behind her, similar to the sound of someone delivering beer barrels. She looked around to see that both Sergeant Huehnergard and Eddie lay deactivated on the ground, rolling slightly.

She turned back to see that the older man was walking unhurriedly towards her. She raised her plastol at his face and squeezed. The gun made a pathetic "whiuwp" noise and died in her hand. She took a couple of steps backwards and unslung the scatter blaster, pumped it once and fired. Nothing. She dropped it on the floor and drew the wickedly curved blade from her belt.

"Let's see you deactivate this," she said as she stepped in and took him under the ribs. The expression on his face betrayed no emotion as she plunged the ceramic blade into his vitals. He hung there in her embrace of death, long enough for the young man to walk behind her. Anne never saw the blow that laid her out. She was slapped on the back of the head, and she went down like a sack of oatmeal.

Mimp

The lighting in the cell came from four ragged filaments embedded in the black fabric of the wall. To Anne's eyes, they resembled glowing fronds of straggly seaweed. She sat cross-legged in the middle of the floor, waiting for her head to clear as her nano-bots worked on the swelling where she had been struck.

She looked around her in the pale red glow of the lighting weed; there was not much to see. The room was conical, like a bell, and as she sat in the silence she attempted to digest the fact that there was no water, no bedding, no food, and most alarmingly, no door for any of the other things to be brought in through.

After a further five minutes of sitting in silence, she realised that there was no air vent either. The cell was completely sealed. This was not a holding area but an oubliette, storage for a soon-to-be corpse.

She stood and began to run her hands over the surface of the wall. She was looking for a seam, or some indication of how they had brought her in. There had to be a door, she reasoned.

With her palms on the smooth black surface of the cell, identical to the material from which the tower she had crashed into was made, she was able to feel an intermittent thudding. Someone on the other side of the wall was banging it.

She leaned forward, trying to tell which direction the noise was coming from, and as she moved, her hand brushed the leather edge of the top of her holster. She looked down, surprised. They had taken her gun but not her belt. With a little smile, she slipped the lace that tied around her thigh, lifting its leather to reveal the flat blade of a ceramic throwing knife.

Experimentally she dug the point into the wall, and just like the tower, the black surface was a thin organic layer, almost like sharkskin, covering a brittle interior.

She began digging chunks out of the wall, heading for the sound of the banging. It was a deep and regular thump, like the sound of a distant door slamming in the wind. Within half an hour she had excavated a hole that was more than a couple of meters deep, and the sound was identifiable as that of fist on wall.

"Who's there?" she hissed when she thought she was close enough.

"Cap'n?" came the startled reply. "Is that you?" The voice of a Blain twin.

"Yeah. Who's that?"

"Philip."

After a further ten minutes of working with a combination of the knife and her bare hands, she broke through into the next cell. As soon as she breached the leathery surface, Philip was able to help by scrabbling at the opening and pulling out handfuls of the material behind.

His cell was identical to hers except it was ten degrees hotter in here, and the lighting weed was in the process of coming away from the wall.

"Richard is down there," said Philip, pointing about forty-five degrees down through the floor. "There's something real wrong with him."

"Don't give me that clone telepathy crap," said Anne sharply, not in the mood for spooky stuff.

"Okay, most clones aren't, but Richard and I aren't standard clones, we're twins. Same vat, same umbilicus, split nucleus, and I'm telling you he's down there. You got any better idea of where to go?"

Anne looked around blankly and blinked, realising that she did not.

"Oké," she said with a shrug, handing him the knife. "Your brother, you dig."

They began excavating a tunnel down in the direction Philip had indicated, crawling on their bellies, pushing the debris out behind them.

Anne was struck by the uncomfortably organic nature of what they were digging through. There was an almost skeletal feel to the structure. The grey material that filled the space between cells was dusty where the knife penetrated it. It crunched like snow whenever any pressure was applied to it, and Anne thought that there was a bone like quality to it

The heat was building as they headed further down.

"I've broken through."

Anne slid through the hole that Philip had made and found him cradling the unconscious body of his brother. The light filament from the wall had come completely free, and where it had fallen on Richard Blain it had enveloped him, merging with his skin.

Richard opened his eyes and looked up at his brother.

"Don't let it touch you. It's the iL'Kizz."

"What iL'Kizz?" whispered Anne. "There haven't been any iL'Kizz for centuries."

"iL'Kizz is not a species, it's a disease."

He appeared to be having trouble swallowing. Philip loosened his brother's shirt, revealing bright red tracks over his skin. They glowed like fresh wounds as his immune system tried in vain to fight the alien invader.

"I can hear its voice. It's like a river flowing through my head, it's washing me away. I know what it knows."

"How do we get out of here then?" Anne cut to the point. Richard tapped the floor of the cell.

"Straight down."

"What do we do about you?" she asked.

Richard stiffened, the sweat on his face glistening in the pale light from the bioluminescence of the strands.

"Take me with you, you bastards, what do you think you do? Easy to cure, just need darkness."

Anne shrugged and, reclaiming the knife from Philip, she began to dig straight down.

The going was a lot slower this time. The material she was digging had to be lifted up and out of the hole. She dug and Philip cleared out the spoil; they had soon excavated a chest-deep pit. An impression she had suddenly formed into words.

"This place is dying."

"Already dead," whispered Richard through clenched teeth.

"Desiccated, like dead leaves. We couldn't work it, didn't have the heart. I have to leave soon. I ... we ... I waited. Needed you to bring it, now I ... we ... I go. It needs time to get strong."

Anne stood up straight to get a good look at Richard, and as she did so the floor beneath her gave way. She fell the last few meters to the deck below. Her landing was neither good nor graceful. She would be carrying the bruises around for a few weeks; however, nothing was broken or sprained.

Philip began to pass his brother down through the hole, the stricken clone weakly grabbing at handholds.

"Leave him, we can't carry him," Anne hissed up at him.

"You might as well be asking me to leave my own leg behind," he hissed back.

"Pah!" she exploded. "Clones!"

However, she took Richard's feet and guided him down to the ground. Philip then lowered himself to where they stood.

They were on what appeared to be a raised roadway, about ten meters wide. There was a sharp cliff of a drop into complete darkness on either side. Set into the curve of the tunnel roof were intermittently spaced glowing clusters of what appeared to be luminescent twigs.

"Where are the PCDs?" Anne asked Richard. Philip had lifted his brother and now supported him, helping him to stand.

"Ship no threat," said Richard. "They left them alone."

"What about the two that came with me? Do you know where they put them?"

Richard screwed his face up in a grimace of mental effort, covering his eyes with the palm of one hand.

"I can see it through them," he sounded surprised. "They left them where they lay."

"Oké," said Anne. "Which way?"

Richard pointed up the walkway. Anne was able to make out a smudge of orange light in the distance.

They set off walking slowly towards what she hoped would be the buildings where the little buggy had been parked. Her plan was simple. Steal a vehicle, head back to the ship, and leave.

Philip was helping Richard to walk, his brother's arm draped around his shoulder. Even in the subdued lighting from the tunnel, Anne could see Richard's face drawn with the effort of the battle that raged within his body.

"What's happening here?" she asked him. "Who are these people?"

At first he did not reply. The question seemed to confuse him.

"I ... they ... we... are the iL'Kizz."

"Captain," said Philip gently. "Let's get him back to the ship first. We can work out the rest when we're safely away from all this."

"I didn't see any iL'Kizz," said Anne, persisting. "All I saw were humans."

"This is iL'Kizz Homeworld. Humans come after the war, and under the sun of the iL'Kizz we took them, made them ours."

The words that Richard spoke were laboured, forced out between breaths, as if merely thinking them was an effort.

"But iL'Kizz without knowledge, without mind."

Anne had lived her entire life on the fringes of human culture. She had heard the name of the iL'Kizz, and vaguely knew that there had been a war with them at some point, but she had no education to draw on, no history.

"Oké," she said. "Let's concentrate on getting out of here."

They walked for a while in silence, heading towards the light. A thought occurred to her.

"If darkness cures it, why are we under cover?"

Richard seemed to be becoming stronger. He was able to walk a little better.

"This was built for the original iL'Kizz species."

As he spoke, his voice grew much clearer and stronger, the words enunciated clearly and without hesitation. "They had a different physiology, different requirements. Human frame much less robust, we need photosynthesis to coexist. We've made some changes to make it more useful."

As he spoke he stood up unaided, taking a step away from his brother.

"Changes?" Anne raised both eyebrows at the concept.

"Yes," said Richard, suddenly seeming fully recovered.

"We had an entire breeding colony of human bodies to play with. After several generations, we were able to make certain improvements."

"Improvements," Anne parroted the word not so much as a question, more as a sort of baffled conversational placeholder.

"Yes," said Richard, stepping away from Philip. "However, you don't have to take our word for it. Judge for yourself, here come a couple now."

He pointed up the tunnel towards the light. Anne could make out movement coming towards them; the shape of limbs rising up but nothing that she was able to see completely. Then, stepping into the circle of light from the illumination cluster above them, she saw what, whatever it was that Richard had become, considered to be an improvement on the human form.

The creature seemed to have been made from human parts, as if someone had attempted a meat jigsaw, without the picture on the box. If Doctor Frankenstein had taken LSD, he might have come up with something similar. The boxy torso had four legs, obviously human, but where they bent at the knee, the thighs hung downwards, suspending the torso in a scorpion-like fashion. It had a human head, at the back of the body on a neck that grew directly up from the creature's chest. There were four arms, two at the back and two at the front, and across its trunk it had several mouths, seemingly arranged at random. They looked like human mouths, except for the scale - they were huge, and when they opened, it was to reveal serrated and jagged looking teeth.

Covering every square centimetre of its naked skin were swirling spirals identical to the tattoo-like markings on the young man that had been their guide. Coming out of the darkness, Anne heard barefoot "pat pat pat" noises as several more of the repellent creatures joined the first.

"These are specialised security units," said Richard calmly. Anne found her gaze drawn hypnotically to the smiling abominations, and the longer her eyes dwelt on their physical horror, the more her stomach wanted to violently expel its contents, one way or the other.

"Shall we continue the way we were going?" said whoever it was that now inhabited the body of Richard Blain. Two of the flesh monstrosities went round behind them and a third took position before them, leading the way.

"What are you going to do with us?" she asked, trying not to look at the random collection of meat parts that seemed to have been sown together by some mad reanimator.

"You have brought something very precious to us," said the Richard thing. "You carry no threat, so it costs us nothing to keep you alive for a while longer."

Behind her, Anne could hear those bare feet, and she shivered despite the stifling heat of the tunnel. She wondered how much damage she would be able to inflict on these creatures with her little throwing knife, and came to the conclusion that it would not be enough.

They walked for a while in silence. Every now and again Anne would steal a glance in Philip's direction. She wondered what he was going through, his clone twin inhabited by another mind. His expression was impassive and stern. He was buttoned up tight as a combat pilot but there was something new in his body language. Anne had known cats as a child, and she recognised in the way that Philip was walking the deliberate steps of a predator looking for an opportunity to fight.

After ten minutes of being led towards the orange light, the tunnel opened out. Anne had expected to be taken back to the buildings that she had first seen but this was a different area.

The great arc of the organic cupola seemed like the dome of a night sky. The very centre of the roof, nearly a kilometre above their heads, was open, a circular aperture that let in a single, wide beam of dust-filled sunlight. The effect was that of a pillar of gold, and at its base hundreds of mirrors caught the light and sent smaller beams back out around the dome to receiving stations that reflected them on even further in little spider's webs.

The main beam looked as if someone had frozen a great golden tornado, and then locked it in with criss-crossing lasers. The slick black buildings, illuminated this way, were lit up with a red-orange glow, and Anne was able to see them, stacked around the edges of the dome like the shelf-toadstools that grew on the trees of New Skye.

At the centre of the golden shaft, the very focus for the pillar of sunlight, was another smaller dome. Richard led them towards it. Anne felt the dread rising with every step. Whenever she had activated the wand, she had always felt this dread. It was as if all the fear that she now felt had somehow leaked across time, and become connected to her whenever she touched the alien metal. This moment was the hub of her life, and the core of her existence was now whatever waited for her within this stygian dome.

She must have stopped for a second, looking up and trying to absorb what she was seeing. She felt a gentle touch on her leg, and looked down to find a hairy hand stroking the inside of her thigh. With a scream she realised that it was one of the flesh beasts. As she turned and backed away from the monstrosity, it grinned at her and every mouth on the beast leered simultaneously.

Philip grabbed her shoulders, and spun her around so that she was no longer looking at the vile creature.

"Keep it together, captain," he hissed.

The word "captain" cut through her panic and snapped her out of it. She had to be the captain, but all she wanted was to be Anne the little girl, with her head under the covers until the monsters went away.

"Yes," she said, and started to walk forwards again. Her legs were like jelly; she could feel the lascivious intent of the monster's gaze as it bore into her back.

Philip put his arm around her shoulder and guided her unwillingly through the fish-mouth arch into the dome. Richard reached a wall and, with a wave, activated it so that it began to fold away into the floor. He turned to Anne and said,

"You have returned our mind to us, our memories and our soul."

Another creature scuttled from the shadows, Anne tried not to look too closely - this one was all arms, all in the wrong places, and far too many of them.

It carried what looked like a black javelin. From the other side, another identical creature came running towards Richard. Anne recognised what it was that this one was carrying.

Held before it as if the most sacred thing in the world, the creature was bearing the metal wand, the treasure map. Anne realised that they must have taken it from her when she lay unconscious.

Richard held out his right hand and the javelin was placed into it, then he held out his left hand and the wand was placed in it.

"It chose well when it chose you, Anne Goldeneyed. We had no way of knowing where it was, all we could do was wait for it to find its own way back."

He placed the wand into the javelin, like a power-clip into a scatter blaster.

"We had to wait, and prepare for when this moment arrived."

The wall was sliding into the ground with a low rumble.

"Our human frames were incapable of creating a body for it, not from one unit, but we have been able to make a home for our heart from our combined flesh."

Anne looked up at the top of the wall that rumbled downwards. Beyond it, Anne could see the golden shaft of sunlight. She could barely breathe and her heart was tapping at the inside of her throat. As the wall slowly dipped out of sight, she could see what lay beyond. At first, she was not able to decode exactly what she was looking at. Then she heard a gasp from beside her as Philip understood. Her eyes refocused, and suddenly her mind gave up its attempt to refuse to understand.

Another dome stood before her, bathed in the golden light of Little Bear. Yet this dome was in the many hues of human skin. Fifty meters across, and all around the edges were bodies, human bodies, packed together, all joined at the back; their arms and legs dangling limp as if dead. Every body had a head, and every head lolled.

The possessed Richard turned to face the amalgam of human components. He pulled back his arm and threw the javelin up into the air. As soon as it left his grasp, a bright beam of orange light snapped out from the roof of the dome, taking the javelin and floating it up and over the organic mound of the human bodies. It hung there for ten seconds, orienting itself directly over the centre of the conjoined mass. The javelin began to spin, and the beam of light that surrounded it changed colour, turning to a dark red.

The vile hump of fused bodies reacted to this. Each mouth began to moan, and beneath the sound they made, another began to build. It was like a thousand reactors going through their ignition cycle, a bass swell that vibrated Anne's flesh from the inside. The power that surrounded the spinning javelin made it vibrate. Anne could feel the terrible noise going through her, trying to crush her.

As the cacophony reached a crescendo, the javelin dropped like a plunged dagger into the very heart of the heap of flesh bodies.

Richard turned to face them, the light of manic triumph blazing in his eyes.

"The iL'Kizz are reborn! We provide the flesh and you have returned to us the personality core of the first iL'Kizz hub mind. Everything it knew, we will know, all it was, we will become. You have awakened us, Anne Goldeneyed, for which we will grant you a swift and painless death."

He began to cross the space towards her and Anne felt herself grasped by unseen hands. She was unable to turn or move. Richard took another step forward and abruptly stopped. A look of confusion crossed his face, and then without a sound he fell face first onto the floor.

Hayties

Anne stood fossil frozen. The fingers of the flesh beasts that grasped her by the arms and legs relaxed their grip, and, gentle as the stroke of lovers' hands, slid from her skin. Where everything had been noise and fury, the space under the dome was now eerily silent.

She was still trying to get her bearings when Philip brushed past her, rushing over to where the unconscious form of his twin lay face down on the ground.

"The old personality is taking over," he said.

"What?" Anne's voice was reedy and uncertain.

Philip looked for a neck pulse and checked pupil dilation. Then, satisfied that his brother was still alive, hoisted him up on his shoulders and started back down the path that approached the focus of the dome.

"That thing was the recorded personality of the most evil thing humanity ever came across in all of the deep-dark, and now it has a new body. I don't know how long we got before it wakes up, but we shouldn't be here when it does.

"Captain, we leave now," he shouted over his shoulder, heading back the way they had come.

Anne stood stock still, transfixed by the sight of the humped mass of human flesh that had been forced together, forming a new body for the preserved mind of the iL'Kizz. It reminded her of a compost heap, made of carrion and corpses. A flash of golden blonde caught her eye, and she realised that she was looking at the hair and face of a young girl that had been welded into this horrifying blob.

As she picked the features of the little girl out from the background, she realised her eyes were open, and that her gaze was being returned. The little girl was awake, and somehow Anne could see her as an individual. There was a look of uncomprehending panic on her face.

As Anne watched, this little wraith began to struggle to get free of the mass of flesh that had taken her individuality, her horror visibly mounting as she realised that she was pressed in by the weight, and connected by skin and nerve to the sweat smelling monstrosity.

Anne could not take her eyes from the girl as her struggle became increasingly desperate. None of the other breathing corpses showed any form of activity, their heads still lolling. Only this one young girl seemed immune to whatever it was that had rendered the rest unconscious.

Anne was already moving forward before she knew what she was doing. The knife appeared in her hand. Suddenly she was running at full pelt towards the great hump of bodies. She leapt up and, using arms and legs as handholds, she climbed, blanking out the horror of what she was doing. She could not think, she must not think. Her foot stood on another neck; she hauled herself past another unconscious face, close as a kiss.

Then she was at the little girl's side.

"It's alright, darling, I'll get you out of here."

"Captain!" Philip Blain's shout was a scream of frustration. "What are you doing? We have to go now."

Anne was stroking the hair of the little girl, trying to find the edges of her body, looking for the place to make the first cut.

When the little girl looked straight into Anne's eyes and spoke, her voice was level, but the terror it contained chilled Anne in a way she had never been touched before.

"The monster is coming."

"I'll get you out of here," said Anne again.

"If you leave now, you can get back to your ship before it wakes up."

The little girl spoke with a lisp, her front two top teeth were missing, but her voice had the weight of maturity. She had been part of the shared identity of the human hive, and knew what it knew.

"I can get you out of here," said Anne. "It's not too late to get you out."

The little girl shook her head with the sadness of reality in the face of Anne's desperation.

"When I wake up … I'm in the nightmare, but I won't be me for long. When the monster comes it will take my mind, and I will sleep again, and it will use me, but I can dream of me free."

"Captain!" screamed Philip. "We need to leave now! Really now!"

Anne looked down at the little girl. Her face looked as if she was falling asleep.

"You have to go before the monster wakes," said the little girl, closing her eyes.

Anne saw her go, and felt as if she was watching someone close to her die in her arms.

"I'll be back for you, Anne," she said softly, unconsciously calling the girl by her own name. "You won't be abandoned. I will always come for you."

The little girl nodded at the words, smiling as she drifted back to her only freedom.

In a blur Anne climbed down and fell, and staggered her way off the hill of bodies. Her shock was getting to the point where she was on the verge of not being able to carry on.

Suddenly Philip was at her side and, with his hand none too gentle in her back, he propelled her back down the path they had come in on.

The body of his twin still over his shoulder, Philip carried Richard in a fireman's lift. They went as fast as they could, until after nearly quarter of an hour of panic-stricken shambling, they exited the tunnel back at the same building that they had come to when they first entered the city.

The lights that had previously bathed the domes and towers of this complex where the humans had been, now fizzled and flashed, stuttering intermittently, lending the scene the animation of firelight. The little orange buggy that they had followed was still parked where the young man had left it.

Unexpectedly, Anne found herself caught in the harsh glare of white headlights.

"Oh there you are, little girl," said Sgt. Huehnergard laconically. "I was beginning to wonder if I'd been scrapped and nobody had told me."

"Philip, grab that buggy and get going."

The arch of daylight that was visible in the distance acted like a stimjet on Anne Goldeneyed. "Sarge, where's Eddie?"

"Right here, sir."

Eddie flashed his headlights to show where he had been hiding in the dark.

"Ok. Pillion, Sarge, and get us back to the *Raven*."

Philip loaded his brother into the open back of the little range buggy and Anne took her place, riding the sergeant as if he were a motorbike.

The buggy started to move off agonisingly slowly. From the edges of her vision, Anne saw movement way above them on the roof of the great city dome. The flickering of the lighting began to stabilise. She heard the words of the little girl.

"The monster is coming."

Here and there as they headed for the entrance Anne could see human forms lying on the ground, and as they came closer and closer to the entrance, she was able to see them beginning to stir.

"Faster, Sarge, Oké? Fast as you can. Get us back to the ship."

"What about the fighters, do you not want to pick them up?"

"Sarge, this is a running away, trying to save our lives situation, just ride will you?"

The sergeant took her at her word and leant forward, putting on the pace until they were flying over the slick black surface of the road. Even the buggy managed to find a little more speed. They powered as fast as they could, racing for the yellow gash of daylight that promised freedom and escape.

"Look!" shouted Philip, pointing up ahead of them.

Anne had already seen it. The fish-mouth arch was closing, like an eyelid being drooped over an empty eye-socket. It moved slowly, a surge of tar ready to engulf them in darkness and death.

The city was rousing itself, righting itself. The awakening mind of the iL'Kizz knew this place of old and was familiar with its organic workings as part of its own body.

Anne could see a change in the black material of the city. Everywhere she looked it had taken on a glistening, almost muscular tone. The road beneath them took on the appearance to her eyes of the tongue of some vast snake, and the walls rippled with sinuous strength. The arch closed slowly before them, and they refused to give up.

"Go for it, Sarge," whispered Anne, her words breathless. She held on tightly to his shoulders, huddling down behind him. The wind against her face grew into a buffeting gale as they reached a hundred and fifty kilometres per hour. Philip had retracted the wheels of the buggy, and it flew now beside the sergeant and Eddie. The sound of the airflow over her ears was deafening, and still the speed built up, and still the great fleshy arch of the city collapsed like a slow waterfall of discarded skin.

Anne could do nothing but watch as the daylight on the road ahead of them slowly diminished, the archway shutting out the golden sun. She was so close to it now that she could see the great curtain of the black skin of the city, unfolding to trap them in its grasp. She tightened her grip on the sergeant's shoulders. Her eyes fixed on the lowering edge of the blackness, and the diminishing yellow stain of daylight reflected in the cobra-skin of the road.

She could hear Philip screaming with rage as he piloted his little buggy straight at the gap. With two centimetres to spare, the buggy shot through the space under the arch, Eddie right on his tail.

"Hold on tight, little girl," shouted the sergeant, diving for the closing gap. He laid himself down sideways, sliding along the surface of the road, protecting Anne's legs with his rear arms, and then the darkness above her was gone. Behind them, and no more than an arms' length away, there was a great sucking impact of flesh on flesh as the arch mated with the road.

Sergeant Huehnergard righted himself and started back to the ship. Anne howled with laughter. She let out a great whoop; her relief was a tidal wave that swept over her.

She looked back at the dome of the iL'Kizz city, and saw that all of the entrances had closed like healed wounds. As they left the darkness of the dome behind them, she could see a change now, sweeping through the army of towers that surrounded the fleeing group. The empty buildings, so long ago abandoned, were coming alive, like sleeping giants, their surfaces rippling and pulsing.

Anne was able to see that what she had thought was a city, was actually a machine. One vast machine that had now been reactivated to house an ancient evil, an evil that she had brought back to it, an evil that now thought of humanity as a resource to be exploited.

They dropped down off the elevated roadway and wound their way at ground level through the maze that led back to their ship, their wake pulling up whirlwinds of blown sand behind them. Eddie took the lead, as his positioning system was still in reliable working order.

A few more minutes of weaving between the eerie alien structures and they came breathlessly to the defensive perimeter that the PCDs of the drop squad had set around the *Raven*.

"Everybody back onboard," she barked. The sergeant did not even slow to take the ramp into the hold. Anne dismounted at the run and, in a series of acrobatic leaps and twists around familiar ladders and banisters, threw herself through the ship until she landed in the catcher's mitt of the pilot's bucket.

Her hands flew over the console. She had to get the ship up and away before the mind in the dome came alive enough to reactivate whatever inhibiting field had killed the *Raven*.

No time for pre-flights, the old bird would have to stretch her wings first time, or die on the ground. Anne felt a deep rumble build in the belly of the ship, followed by the erotic whine of the starter turbines spinning up to speed. A heavy clunk reverberated through the fabric of the ship as Sergeant Huehnergard raised the belly ramp. Philip Blain shouted up from the hold.

"Everyone on board. Go, go go."

Anne opened the fluidic injectors to full, and heavily the old shuttle let go her grip on the ground. She rose, unsteadily at first, up through the dead air of the tower. Anne turned on the headlights and could see structures welling up on the inside of the building, as if the skin was extruding components.

Sliding down a runner from somewhere near the peak of the spire, she saw a drum-shaped projector, like the ones that had caught her in the holding beam, descending the wall towards her.

"This time I got guns!" she muttered to herself, thumbing the trigger guard on her flight controller. The drum centred itself level to the ship. With a grim smile Anne squeezed the trigger.

From beneath the stubby wings of the *Raven*, two heavy bore beam weapons ripped space apart into random chaos. Without the protection of the dampening field that had paralysed the *Raven* the first time, the iL'Kizz tractor-projector exploded, and the wall behind was blasted into hypersonic gobbets. Anne fired again, opening the hole further.

With a mighty roar from the manoeuvring thrusters, she brought the throttle up to full, and the old bird threw herself towards and out through the gap. She was skyborne once again.

Anne set the nose towards the heavens, kicked in the main thrust and the *Raven* streaked away; reaching for orbit the way a drowning person reaches for the riverbank.

Behind her, on the ground, something was happening to the newly awakened city. Eddie had set the sensors to sweep the dome and the surrounding towers, looking for any possible pursuit.

"I really think you should take a look at this, captain," he said, putting the feed through to her position.

On the surface of Little Bear, waves of colour were passing over the city, like ripples spreading out from the central point of the great dome. Anne found her eyes drawn to the movement. There was something uncomfortable about what she was looking at. The colours were from the rainbow of rot. As her gaze was held fascinated by the almost insect-like peristalsis that throbbed across the city, the great dome began to fade, becoming transparent.

A dreadful misgiving crossed her mind. Anne swirled through the telemetry settings and, as she suspected, massive transphasic emissions were phase shifting the whole city, changing the quantum base note of its reality. The iL'Kizz was fleeing from the universe.

She had not been able to detect the city when she had first arrived because these human iL'Kizz drones had found a way to push it outside the normal boundaries of reality, and now it was heading back into this extra-universal space. Like the Sandlions of New Skye, this foul thing was digging in.

Anne realised then that it was letting her go because it did not need to catch her today; there would always be a tomorrow for it. She also realised, lying back in the pilot's throne, just what it was that she had brought back to life on Little Bear.

By the time the *Raven* had docked with *The Morrigan*, there was no sign on any of the sensors that there had ever been a city. It had gone.

Philip took his brother straight to the med-bay, and Anne walked slowly onto the bridge.

"I've laid in course for nearest crumple, sir," said Nancy Kurita, hovering over the flight controls. "Say word and I have us on way out system."

Anne looked up, green steel in her eyes, and the face of a small girl in her mind.

"No," she said. The word was flat, non-negotiable, and vehement.

"I still have business here."

Sayties

Anne sat in darkness. She was leaning back in her armchair; legs outstretched and booted ankles crossed. She seemed to be looking down at the face of Little Bear, but her gaze was without focus and turned inward.

In her right hand she absent-mindedly spun a Tibetan prayer-wheel, and in her left she snuggled her favourite room-cleaner, a Patet Segal NC-6040 plastol, with over-and-under field inverters and adjustable phase lock.

There was music to match her brooding. She had selected the neo-gothic cantatas of Alba Fides, written before the first Scorpius war, and cranked them up so loud that she could see her window vibrating under the huge swell of the bass.

Five standard weeks had passed since she had escaped the city, and the crew were becoming restive. Anne had had to spend most of the last hour speaking to Sir January of Orkney and Knuth Silverhand, the masters of the *Epona* and the *Hecate*. She could feel their impatience growing as each new day passed without profit.

Knuth was from Jotunheim in the Nine Worlds Confederation, and Anne reckoned that he was simply bored. A little action would probably be enough to get him back on side.

She smiled as she brought his shaggy features to mind. Knuth was never really happy unless the air around him boiled with plasma.

The bigger problem as she saw it lay with Sir January and her blasted "quest".

Anne turned her gaze to the prayer wheel and spoke as if to another person.

"Never do business with a religious nut," she said. "You never know what the voices in their head are going to tell them to do next." However, it was the little voice in her own head that was the proving to be more of a problem.

Each time she closed her eyes she would see a shock of blonde hair and piercing blue eyes. Eyes that were old with pain and inappropriate knowledge. She cocked the gun again, longing for a target that would set her soul free.

An irritating buzz created a discordant undertone to Anne's thoughts. The sound steadily grew in insistency until it finally cut through her mental fug, and she realised that someone was at the door. With a gesture she silenced the music and, laying her prayer wheel aside, got up and palmed the lock.

Nancy Kurita drifted in with a tray.

"I told you, when I want to eat I'll get it myself," said Anne, more tired than genuinely irritated.

"We not leave here until you find city, yes?" asked Nancy by way of reply.

"Yes," said Anne. "That is exactly right. We not leave here until then." She cocked the plastol to emphasise the point.

"Okay then," said Nancy. "I have way of bring back city. You need eat first, then I tell you how." Anne looked over the contents of the tray, and realised she could eat a bite. She took it from the PCD's hands and plonked herself back down in her armchair.

"I eat, you talk," she said around a mouthful of crispy Angel Hair.

"From emission signature," began Nancy, projecting the telemetry recorded during the *Raven*'s escape, "the city of iL'Kizz is simple phased. Translated, not translocated. She still there, hovering above perceivable dimensions. Easy."

"I know that already," said Anne, wiping her chin with her hand. "What I don't know is how to force it back, Oké?"

Nancy laid her RF aerial flat over her head.

"String storm," she said simply. Anne slurped from her bowl and chewed thoughtfully in silence for nearly half a minute.

"I am assuming you are going to tell me what that is, and exactly how to make one."

"There's the hard part," said Nancy.

"I kind of thought it would be."

*

Eleven drop pods were down on the surface, their positions all within the margin for error that Mr Kurita had allowed for. Anne Goldeneyed stood on the bridge of her Morrigan, the main viewer displaying a close up of the area where the city had disappeared. Philip Blain was ready in the pilot seat, and Nancy Kurita was settling herself in at the weapons console.

"Take us in," Anne ordered.

The nose of *The Morrigan* dipped towards the planet and with a blue glow the main drive fired up. They were going in on the daylight side, and at first the old ship barely seemed to move in comparison with the mass of Little Bear.

Nancy Kurita's plan had been neither simple nor without danger. After analysing the data and sensor logs from the *Raven*, Nancy realised that what had brought the shuttle down, and also knocked out the Sarge and Eddie, had been a simple neutron dampening field. This was a technology that had been obsolete by the end of the iL'Kizz war.

Nancy's Personality Donor had built something similar in her second year of college, and that had been nearly a hundred and fifteen years earlier. Ten minutes with a tuning coil and a spanner had been enough to render the ships' phase shields immune to it.

Puzzled by the age of the technology, Nancy had gone back over the recordings of the transphasic bursts that had moved the iL'Kizz city into phase space. The energy signature was also antique, same as the dampening field.

Anne was no mathematician, and it had taken Mr Kurita nearly twenty minutes of patient explanation of the basics of low dimensional topology to explain that the iL'Kizz could only have translated the city's co-ordinates within the dimensions of a Kaluza-Klein hyperspatial bottle.

Eventually Anne had grasped what that meant. Although the city had been translated out of the apparent universe, it had not moved. It was merely hiding. Nancy had devised a way of flushing it out.

Cosmological topology was a required skill for any navigator, and Nancy was a good one. She knew that the fundamental jigsaw piece, from which the great picture of the universe was composed, was a string. A structure so unimaginably small, it exists only in the spaces where any form of scale or dimension are meaningless concepts.

Nancy also knew that strings and super strings have one thing in common, that if enough momentum can be imparted to them, as they move they create space behind them.

A string bomb had always been pointless, because strings barely react with baryonic matter. However if your enemy was in the universe next door, then a burst of uncountable trillions of strings flung out of this universe, each trailing little bits of space, would be like an almost infinite number of infinitesimally small daggers, tearing apart anything hiding in phase space. Like a nail bomb through a bed-sheet.

When Nancy had outlined the plan, Anne had spotted the problem.

"But we don't have a string bomb."

"That where it get a little difficult," Nancy admitted. "No string bomb, but I work out how to start string-storm. Need all our drop pods, and eleven fusion bombs, and we have to be closer to planet than this crap old ship can manage. Then even if it work and iL'Kizz come back, what we do then?"

"We destroy the brain," snapped Anne sharply. "We put her out of her misery."

Anne had never been one for self analysis, but even she had had to ask herself why she was doing this. She had always made a point of never taking anything personally. It was how she had survived the abuses of her childhood, it had been what had enabled her to slit the throat of her owner and make her own way amongst the stars.

Yet somehow what the personality core of the iL'Kizz had done to her, infecting her mind, trying to pollute her body with its invasive filth, she took that personally. It had tried to make her a slave again, tried to replace her will with its own, and no force in the universe was going to get away with that.

The eyes of the little girl bore into her soul like twin blue laser beams, cutting through her heart. She could not let her go. The little girl was no different to how she had been, locked into a life of connected slavery; unable to move because of the press of the vast bulk of fleshy humanity weighing down on her. Anne had cut herself free, with a single stroke to a human throat. Yet now there was nowhere she could cut to free the little girl.

Reluctantly and slowly, against every emotion inside her, Anne had eventually come to the conclusion that the only freedom she could offer was the freedom of death. She had to kill the hub-mind. She had to destroy the abomination of stolen flesh, and make sure that no other souls were consumed by its alien hunger.

The PCDs had spent the next three days removing the warheads from ship-to-ship missiles and installing them into the drop pods. The pods were released, and Anne had watched them with satisfaction as they penetrated the atmosphere of the planet, setting down one by one.

The Morrigan needed to get within range of her main phased array. That range and the minimum orbital altitude were very close to being the same. The *Epona* and the *Hecate* had taken up flanking positions, and accompanied the larger ship into the outer limits of the atmosphere.

Anne stood on the bridge, listening to the RF chatter from the PCDs as they monitored the descent. She watched Philip Blain as his hands flew over the consoles, keeping the old ship balanced against the pull of Little Bear.

A new emotion began to tug at the belly of Anne Goldeneyed. It had started, she was going in, and an unknown enemy waited for her. She found herself wondering what she was doing there. Her train of thought was broken by a flashing alarm, indicating that external sensors had detected gas ionisation. It had started, and there was no going back from it.

"Target lock acquired on the first drop pod," announced Nancy Kurita. "Two minutes to effective firing range."

"Keep us on approach."

The ship began to shake slightly. Anne could feel it through the decking as a deep rumble. *The Morrigan* was never designed with atmospheric entry in mind. Anne kept an eagle eye on the shield status. It was only the field generators that were keeping the old coloniser vessel from erupting into a disintegrating comet of human fire.

She looked over at the two vessels that flanked her. Both were sleek, with aerodynamic designs. The golden gases of re-entry trailed from their wing tips like streamers of boiling metal.

The shaking that seized *The Morrigan* became more violent for a second. Anne fell back into the command seat and activated the restraining field. She looked over anxiously to where Philip Blain sat. The concentration in his eyes made his face shine with a manic expression. His implants were allowing him to react to the data from the ship faster than an unaugmented human would ever have been capable of, but for the first time Anne wondered if even his tricked out systems would be enough to keep her home in one piece against the forces of Little Bear.

The shaking came back down a notch. Philip's shoulders relaxed the merest fraction, but it was enough to let Anne know that he had regained control.

"One minute to effective range," announced Nancy Kurita. She had to turn up her voice synth to the level of a shout in order to be heard over the creaking of the stress members as *The Morrigan* flexed under the strain.

With a wave of her hand, Anne summoned the images of Knuth and Sir January.

"We're holding," she said. "Begin your run."

Knuth nodded silently and disappeared. Sir January genuflected and kissed her thumbnail before severing the connection. Anne saw the two ships aim themselves toward the planet. With a brief glow they set their phase shields for atmospheric insertion, and then swooped away like stooping falcons. Within a few seconds they were merely dots on the screen, heading out from *The Morrigan* and racing away from each other at their best pace.

"Thirty seconds to effective range."

"Status?" Anne barked across at Philip Blain.

"Structural integrity is within predicted parameters," he answered. "We can hold this for a few minutes yet, and still have enough thrust to get us back out of the gravity well."

"Coming up on the first drop pod in ten seconds," shouted Nancy.

"Charge the main array," responded Anne. Throughout the ship the atmosphere crackled with static as the phase generators built to firing capacity. The sharp smell of electrified air cut through the atmosphere on the bridge, bringing Anne to a new level of wakening. Her mind suddenly focused and slipped into the timeframe of battle.

"Detonation of warhead one," announced Nancy, and as she spoke she fired the main array. Lightning lit up the inside of Anne's head. The great gun of *The Morrigan* illuminated everything in Anne's reality with a blast that reached across dimensions.

On the surface of the world below, the first warhead detonated in a maximum yield fusion blast. The white hot flash curled up, a toy star, and then slicing down from *The Morrigan* came a pillar of crackling fury spat from the heavens, overdriving the fusion process, tearing apart the very fabric of space-time, releasing the energy of the material structure of the universe.

The Morrigan then tracked the incandescent shaft of weapons fire over the surface of Little Bear, like a rapier dragged across skin, to the second drop pod, and the third, and on until eleven suns burned on the surface of the world.

The material of space began to degrade, unable to accommodate energy of such a scale, the combination of phase and thermo-nuclear weapons oscillating the flat surface of existence, cleaving the canvas on which everything is painted. No longer able to contain the fury of the assault, the brane of this universe began shedding energy in a transdimensional stringplosion.

Nancy Kurita's storm began, a wound in space bleeding reality, haemorrhaging out across the neighbouring dimensions as shrapnel made of infinitesimal scalpels of expanding space.

"That's it," Anne shouted. "Get us clear, Philip."

Philip Blain initiated a turn and a simultaneous roll, pointing the nose of *The Morrigan* back towards the darkness and safety of space. The old vessel screeched under the stresses of the full throttle manoeuvre. The shaking of the deck mounted as she took the strain in the struggle against the gravity of the planet below.

Anne was almost overwhelmed by the noise, and the violence of the ride. She had never heard her ship scream like this. The engine howled like tortured demons, a piercing turbine whine that penetrated, sharp as a drill through her brain. The lighting on the bridge began to fade to an orangey glow as the propulsion system grabbed power from low priority systems.

On the surface of the planet, in the midst of the storm that raged across the dimensions, a dark patch appeared upon the awesome light. It grew, taking form, first as a line, and then slowly the line turned around its axis, forming a circle, which then turned once again, becoming a sphere, which turned again, becoming a door.

Beyond the door, Anne could see the dome of the city. It emerged from the sea of fire like the black focus of everything evil. Born from this conflagration, the iL'Kizz struggled from the furnace. The city was now visible in its entirety.

The optical sensors were almost overwhelmed by the luminosity of the fusion storm that raged below, but Anne could make out changes in the dark silhouette of the great dome. Huge spires had erupted around the edges of the tegument, giving the whole thing the appearance of a great black crown.

Anne could see the fires of the warheads beginning to die back as the energy of the string storm abated. The city looked ragged and tattered. The forest of towers was gone, only here and there did the occasional structure rise from the sands. The dome itself, however, seemed to have been untouched. It still sat like a malevolent eye, staring up at the universe.

Inside *The Morrigan* the screaming of the turbines abated, and the noise levels began to drop back to the normal background hum. Anne could hear the RF chatter of the PCDs as damage control teams reported in.

"Here they come," said Nancy flatly.

The deadly shapes of the *Epona* and *Hecate* raced in over the desert, intent on delivering the coup-de-grace. They hugged the ground low, phase shields set forward, charging in on full throttle.

The hub mind had obviously detected them and reacted. Several of the spires around the edge of the dome blasted off, revealing their true nature as chemical lifting bodies. Anne could see them on the main viewer, each belching a column of fire that hurled them into the heavens. At first she thought they were missiles aimed at her or the frigates, but as they reached a critical altitude they engaged a secondary propulsion system and soared towards the heavens, and Anne realised from their track that they were escape vessels.

She had a sudden image of a seed pod bursting, scattering spores to the winds.

"All gunnery crews, weapons free," she ordered. "Repeat weapons free. Don't let them get past us."

The Morrigan's deadly arsenal erupted into life over the hull of the ship. Another wave of spires blasted off from the main dome. The *Epona* and *Hecate*, on converging tracks, were now in range, and they began to fire up at the departing ships. Together they reached the edge of the city and began a steep climb, heading back for space.

As they reached safe altitude, the two ships simultaneously launched their payloads. Anne's remaining stock of missiles had been plundered and stripped of their warheads to make two fusion weapons capable of reducing the entire structure of the iL'Kizz dome to nothing but atoms.

Anne watched breathlessly as the dome split like the segments of an orange, the covering of the city beneath shucked off and blown away like cardboard by something inside. From the very centre of the dome a dark shape began to rise towards space, taking off, trying to avoid the detonation of the thermo-nukes. Anne was just able to see it clearing the ground, struggling to get into the air, when the optical sensors where overwhelmed by the twin blasts of the two h-bombs.

For four painful seconds *The Morrigan* was blind until the sensors gradually faded back in. The city was gone. On the surface of the planet nothing but devastation and the angry orange of hellish flame and smoke that reached up in a rapidly cooling mushroom cloud. Yet Anne was no longer concerned about that.

"Did you get track on the main ship? Was it destroyed or did it get away?" she barked.

"There it is!" shouted Nancy Kurita. The iL'Kizz escape ship was headed straight for them. Anne could see it as a tiny dot on the viewer, rising furiously from the planet.

"Designate target one, concentrate all weapons, open fire."

Anne felt the white cold rage of battle.

"Can you get a shot with the main array?" she called across to Nancy.

"Two minutes to recharge, we don't have time."

Every weapon on the ship turned to meet the threat rising from Little Bear. Philip rotated *The Morrigan* to allow the heavier blast cannon on the rear to get a clear shot. Beam after raking beam lanced out at the iL'Kizz, but the organic looking seed of the escape ship was heavily shielded. *The Morrigan* might as well have been armed with soft-light weapons for all the impact they were making.

"The ship is clear of the atmosphere," announced Philip Blain. "Still coming straight for us."

Anne looked at the incoming vessel.

"Very well," she said quietly to her self. "We'll go together, shall we?"

"Philip," she shouted. "Bring us around so we're sharp end on. Let's see if we can't skewer the bastard."

As the iL'Kizz ship cleared the atmosphere it found a crumple and deployed a D-probe. Suddenly the escape ship picked up speed and came thundering directly towards *The Morrigan*.

"Brace for collision," Anne ordered, but the impact never came.

At the last possible moment the iL'Kizz ship rolled to one side and passed between *The Morrigan* and the planet. The distance between the two vessels no more than twenty meters.

At the closest point the iL'Kizz ship opened up with a single deep blue beam, which wrapped around the hull of *The Morrigan*. Every system aboard the old ship blew like a cheap fuse in a lightning storm.

The bridge was suddenly plunged into complete darkness, which was replaced a few seconds later by beams of white as Nancy Kurita turned on her headlights. Anne sat waiting for the next shot, the one that would tear *The Morrigan* into shreds of orbital scrap.

After thirty seconds, the continuous sound of muttered swearing coming from

Mr Kurita as she tried to reconnect the main power entered her consciousness, and she realised that the one shot was all the iL'Kizz had. She stood and left the bridge, and went down to her cabin. From the window she could still see the bright dot of the alien ship as it caught the sun.

As she watched, the escaping hub-mind opened a crumple, just like it had done at Faker's Head. Powerless to do anything, Anne looked on as the eater of souls simply disappeared.

Lightning Source UK Ltd.
Milton Keynes UK

176648UK00001B/47/P

9 780956 392404